UNFINISHED DREAMS

a novel by

Jane Breskin Zalben

SIMON & SCHUSTER
BOOKS FOR YOUNG READERS

SIMON & SCHUSTER BOOKS FOR YOUNG READERS
An imprint of Simon & Schuster Children's Publishing Division
1230 Avenue of the Americas, New York, New York 10020
Copyright © 1996 by Jane Breskin Zalben
SIMON & SCHUSTER BOOKS FOR YOUNG READERS
is a trademark of Simon & Schuster.

Book design by Jane Breskin Zalben
The text for this book is set in Palatino.
Printed and bound in the United States of America
First Edition
10 9 8 7 6 5 4 3 2 1

Library of Congress Cataloging-in-Publication Data
Zalben, Jane Breskin.
Unfinished dreams : a novel / by Jane Breskin Zalben. p.   cm.
Summary: Jason, a nine-year-old Jewish boy, pursues his dream
of becoming a great violinist, even as he deals with disappointments
and the deaths of loved ones.
ISBN 0-689-80033-9 (hc)
1. Jews—United States—Juvenile fiction.   [1. Jews—United States—Fiction.
2. Violin—Fiction.   3. Schools—Fiction.   4. Death—Fiction.]   I. Title.
PZ7.Z254Un   1996   [Fic]—dc20   95-44424

Acknowledgments

❦

I wish to thank my son, Jonathan Zalben, for the inclusion of poems he wrote at ages ten and eleven, within the text, and for the painting he did after a class trip to a Matisse show, and the Mozart puppet, which appear on the jacket cover photo. I want to let him know how much it has touched me to watch over the years his long-distance friendship with his best friend, Caleb Hodes. Cudos to Alexander Zalben's Schreiber Lampoon for the song, "Single Cells." I would also like to thank Trish Baehr in my writing group, and my editor, Stephanie Owens Lurie, whose comments I respect. And lastly, the many people who have guided my son's way: the principal, who once thought enough to single him out and allow him to keep a violin under the desk in his office; Joseph Mooney and José Sanchez, who showed him the way and continue to inspire him; and Margaret Pardee, at The Juilliard School, who's guiding him there, with appreciation.

To Jonathan—
who brings music every day into my life.
I wish you the world.

"... to be born into this world exactly the way it is, into these exact circumstances, even if that meant not having a dad or an ozone layer, even if it included pets that would die and acne and seventh-grade dances and AIDS."

Anne Lamott, Operating Instructions

UNFINISHED DREAMS

September

❦

Why can't life be like a Disney cartoon, where dreams come true and everyone lives happily ever after? That's what went through my mind on the first day of sixth grade, when my teacher, Mrs. Jackson, said, "I'd like all of you to make a wish list. We'll look at it now, and again at the end of the year. You'd be surprised how your wishes can change over time."

I took a piece of paper from my loose leaf. Wendy Weins tapped her pencil up and down. Tommy Wachowski kicked Wendy's chair. Then the only sounds in the classroom were scribbling and throat clearing, mainly by Barney Rosenthal, who has asthma. Finally, I wrote wish number one: *I wish that my pets could live forever.*

Yesterday, my rabbit, Sniffles, died. She had been sick for months. While Mom called the vet, I went in the backyard and stretched out on Grandpa Sy's old army blanket next to Sniffles, nose to nose, feeling her shallow breaths and frail body beside me. I kissed her three paws. The right front one had been amputated weeks before. She crawled closer and fell because she could no longer hop. I placed her on my chest. Mom took pictures to remember her by. Then she gave her a bath, as she had done every day lately because Sniffles got so messy. Mom used the blow-dryer on her thick black fur as I held her on my lap. I prayed she'd get better. When she didn't, I wanted her to die peacefully, but she kept hanging on. It was the hardest decision I had to make in my entire life: to put her to sleep or not.

The veterinarian gave her a shot in her heart. Afterward, I held Sniffles until she became limp in my arms. It was the first time I'd seen anything dead. It was difficult for me to even think about letting go of someone I loved so much. But I had to. For her. We buried her in the yard, wrapped in her favorite pale blue towel, the terry cloth worn and chewed through. I carefully placed her ball into the deep hole. It jingled one last time as I helped my father shovel in the dirt. My mother cried. My father put his arms around her. My four-year-old brother, David, wedged his way between them. We put rocks in a circle around the grave, as though the circle would protect her. It rained on Sniffles last night. I listened to the patter outside my bedroom window, and as I stared at the glow-in-the-dark crescent moon and stars on my ceiling, I knew I would check on her after I got off the school bus today. To make sure the stones remained. I wondered if I should dig the ball back up. Would I miss seeing it? Her nudging it with her nose like a dog, hearing the bell inside the ball as she hopped around her hutch in our kitchen. Most of all, I wanted her to lick me with her warm, smooth tongue. To be alive. And furry. And here. I simply wanted her here.

Caleb Harmon is the only friend who understands how I feel about Sniffles. His Scottish terrior, Franklin, is older than Caleb and can barely walk. Caleb says, "If you multiply my age times seven, that's about how old Franklin is, which makes him over eighty-four in dog life."

I was going to miss hanging out with Caleb and doing whatever we wanted. So wish number two would be: *I wish that summer had lasted longer*.

Caleb's back porch had become our personal laboratory. He and I collected tadpoles and minnows. We put them in peanut butter jars and punched holes in the lids. There were always jars leftover after we caught fireflies and then released them as twilight became night. We also had bugs crawling on leaves and salamanders slithering on rocks in terrariums. In a glass fishbowl, we kept a frog we found in the millpond. We named it "Pinky" because its belly seemed so pale. Caleb and I have been finding things and doing projects since we were five.

Mrs. Harmon said to us, "If you two boys ever

roomed together, I'd open the closet door and an avalanche would fall on my head!"

Summer also meant staying over at Grandma Fanny's. I love her even though the minute she sees me she hugs me too tight. When I back away, she often says, "I forget that eleven's too old for a hug." I blush, look up a tiny bit, because we're almost the same height now, and she kisses me near my forehead, and winks. "No one's ever too old for a hug," she says.

Now that summer is over, I'll miss Grandma's cooking every day. She loves that I love her cooking. Especially her rice pudding with plump raisins and cinnamon sprinkled on top. She thinks I'm her number one fan. I'll never tell her I really prefer Dad's cooking, but then maybe he gets his talent from her. I'll also miss the sheets on her beds. When I crawl in at night after a hot day at the beach, they are the cleanest and coolest sheets in the whole world. From my room, I can see morning glories twisting up the white trellis on the side of the bungalow—how bright blue they are—and I know this sounds so corny—but they are beautiful, like the sky and the water. They remind me of summer now gone.

Summer wasn't so great for Mr. Carr, our principal. At the town pool, where he loved to do laps every day, I overheard that he was sick. I wondered why I hadn't seen him there. Since I was in kindergarten, on the first day of Sherman Elementary School, Mr. Carr shook every child's hand as we

4

got off the school bus. That very first day, when he grabbed my hand and held it in his large, warm palm, I felt as if it would be okay in this big building. Today was the first time ever he wasn't out there shaking everyone's hand and telling his dumb puns, like the one about pigs dancing *Swine Lake*, or that his pet fish was a Phi Beta Snapper. Groan. Groan. It was his idea to start small group recitals in the school system; I dreamed of being in one this year. Wish number three would definitely be: *Come back, Mr. Carr. Please.*

Mrs. Jackson went around the classroom asking about our dreams. She called, "Jason Glass, do you have any thoughts on the subject?" I paused and answered, "Someday I'd like to play in the New York Philharmonic Orchestra."

Tommy Wachowski yelled out, "And I'd like to play for the Mets."

That was when I realized my fourth wish would be: *I wish that Tommy wasn't in my class this year.*

I didn't always want to be a violinist. When I was six years old, I wanted to play the bagpipes. Don't ask me why, I just did. It certainly wasn't the kilts. Wearing a skirt and kneesocks wasn't a big draw. Grandma Fanny had said, "Who ever heard of a Jewish boy playing the bagpipes?" But my parents took me to see a policemen's band, anyway, and the chief let me try a chanter. So I wanted to be a policeman. My grandmother said, "Darling, pick a safe profession."

In third grade, we had to choose an instrument. Somehow, bagpipes weren't up there on the top ten list. As I passed over the cello and the clarinet, to me the violin was about the closest sound you could get to the bagpipes, so I signed up for group lessons in school. After my parents were told by Mr. Carr that I showed "a real facility" for the instrument, I had asked, "Could I have private lessons?" They answered, "First let's see if you're serious. No one in the entire family has ever played the violin. You're the only one." That settled that. I would do something that was *all mine.*

After six months, I began half-hour lessons in the basement of Larry's Music World. I squeaked out tunes in a tiny cubicle, between piano lessons pounding on one side and drums beating on the other. "This is no way to learn," my mother had said. So that summer, before the beginning of fourth grade, she asked Juan, who had started playing in my parents' restaurant on Saturday nights when he needed extra money, to give me longer lessons. He goes to The Juilliard School. Full scholarship. He, too, dreamed of being a violinist.

Just as class ended, I wrote wish number five: *I wish someday, maybe I'll audition for Juilliard.*

Inside I knew that would always really be wish number one.

The house was empty when I got home from school. Mom was probably still at the restaurant and David at his sitter's. Since I had a lesson later today, I took my bow out of the case standing next to my bed to rosin it. For Chanukah last year, I got a small box of special rosin. The purple-black cake was nestled in a tiny cotton cloth and glistened when I opened the lid. My bow was in the style of ones made by Tourte, a famous bow maker. "Yours was probably made by an apprentice of his," said Mr. Grinaldi, the man we had bought it from. He makes violins in the dark, cluttered basement of his house. There wasn't even a buzzer on the back door to let us in and out. "We can just walk in?" I had whispered to my parents after we did.

My violin is German. Mittenwald. 1910. The store owner showed us the papers documenting the date, just like the breeder who had sold Wendy Weins her white French poodle. The owner's father had made bows for Itzhak Perlman and Isaac Stern. There were several with ivory tips, which is rare because ivory is so scarce and not allowed to be used anymore. The ivory comes from elephant's tusks, and I'm glad there's a ban on killing them.

Dad had said, "We bought oppositely. The bow should have been from the bow maker, and the violin from the violin maker." But I fell in love with each separately. I liked the feel and light weight of the bow, and the sound of the violin. And how the two came together, making music.

I tightened the bow just the right amount, leaving a space the thickness of a pencil between the hair and stick, and began. Sometimes it takes me awhile to get into the music, like today. But when it is going well, I feel as though I am not even there. I am somewhere else, in between, suspended. There are times I erase all sounds other than the notes: the distant vibrations of the boiler, the fish tank in my room, or the outdoor noises from the street. That is when I am really into the music. Mom tells me, "You purse your lips when you play." Dad says, "Your eyebrows go up and down while you sway to the rhythm." I don't know what I do. All I know is how I feel, and that is happy and alive and peaceful when I am playing.

When I finally looked up at the clock it was almost two hours later. My mother's voice came from the direction of the kitchen as David slammed the back door. "Jason? Jason, honey, we're home."

"In here," I shouted back.

I set the violin in its case and opened my bedroom door. David was waiting for me, dangling a rubber spider. "I'm real scared," I said, and pretended to faint. David seemed pleased about frightening me, so I played dead as he lifted one of my eyelids.

"Are you okay? Jason?" He put his ear to my heart.

I held my breath, sat straight up like vampires

do in those horror movies when their coffins open, and yelled, "Boo!"

"Mommy!" David whined as he ran into the kitchen where my mother was heating dinner. I followed him grudgingly. She ignored us, knowing we were up to our usual routine. I thought of wish number six: *I wish that David would disappear.* Just kidding. Well, half-kidding.

"How was school today?" Mom asked, handing me the salad.

"Okay."

"Do you like your teacher?"

"She's okay."

"A man of many words," Mom said as I wolfed down her homemade ravioli in pesto sauce. Then we all got in the car to go to my lesson. David napped in the back car seat as soon as the car began to move.

After the half-hour drive to Westbury, Mom dropped me off in front of the house where my new teacher, Mrs. Lee, lives. David stirred when the car stopped. His head bounced a few times and then dropped back into a deep sleep as he let out a snort. "Have a good lesson," Mom said softly.

"Okay." I shrugged.

Mrs. Lee goes to Venezuela every June to find students and bring them back to the United States. Then she teaches them until they are good enough to enter Juilliard. She's been teaching there for over fifty years. Juan is one of her "finds." She discovered him, a homeless teenager, singing with his *cuartro* on the street. He hoped that as I advanced, she'd teach me. She took me on this summer. It was the best graduation gift I could have gotten at the end of fifth grade!

Over the years, many of Mrs. Lee's students have lived in her house, coming and going, doing odd chores and mowing the overgrown lawn in exchange for room and board. As I rang the front doorbell I heard strains of arpeggios mixed with Mozart and Bach coming from various bedrooms. Ricardo, a friend of Juan's, let me in, and then went back to the kitchen to get Mrs. Lee. As I tried to find a space to stand between the books and music scores piled high on the stained yellow carpet, I heard her say to him, "How many hours did you practice today?"

"Three," he mumbled, opening up the refrigerator door.

"Do more," she scolded. "Get up earlier. It's not enough."

I prepared my bow and tuned my violin to the A on her grand piano, wondering, how did the movers fit the piano through the narrow front door? How will it be taken out someday? In pieces? Vases filled with wilting roses, and dried, crumbling bouquets, leftover from concerts of her many students, were on top of the piano, next to her sleeping cat.

"Warm up," Mrs. Lee called in to me.

I arranged the sheets of my scale exercises on the old wooden music stand. At home, mine is aluminum, portable, and wobbles when I play. A pencil hangs from a string attached to her stand, which I use to circle my mistakes. *I* circle them, not her, so that *I* remember them.

As I played my scales I glanced around the living room. Every square inch holds an object. Teacups, dolls, and rows of figurines from all over the world, places she must have toured, are covered with dust and crammed on shelf after shelf. Framed photographs of students, some younger than David, posed, holding tiny violins. It made me feel that I had started studying seriously too late at nine years old. A small lamp cast dim light onto paintings done by Mrs. Lee's husband before he had Alzheimer's disease. From the finished basement I heard the woman who takes care of Mr. Lee scream, "Eat! Eat!" That upset me. The thought of getting old, sick, and unable to play. Or maybe even to listen. For some reason, I missed Sniffles all over again. The feeling came in waves.

Mrs. Lee came in, sat in her comfortable red chair, raised her feet on an ottoman, and placed a cup of tea on the stack of music.

"Ah-h-h," she sang along with me. "Have you been doing your scales an hour a day?"

"Yes." My palms sweated, knowing I did less sometimes.

"Play a hard one for me. In three octaves."

I played a G-sharp minor scale.

"Better intonation," she winced.

I played it again.

11

"Cleaner. Clearer." She thumped her hand on the arm of the chair, showing me the rhythm. "Watch your bowing arm. Closer to the bridge."

I did the scale another time.

"Be careful of the direction of the frog. Have you been doing your Dont études?" I fumbled for my book. "I don't want to hear them. I want to know are you *doing* them?"

I smiled awkwardly. "Yes."

"Good." She trusts me more than my parents do. But then she would really know if I hadn't done them.

"Let's hear the Haydn." I took out the Concerto in G Major. I'd been practicing it for two months. "Can you play it without the music?"

"I think so." I hoped my memory was good. I was afraid as I began the first movement.

Her foot moved back and forth on the ottoman, keeping the beat like a metronome. "No," she said at a measure. "Look at the music. Forte. Give it strength. More vibrato. Your fingers are too tense. Loosen up."

I began again, trying to intensify the notes without being tense.

"Here," she pointed, "a quarter note."

Carefully I continued, until she stopped me.

"And again," she interrupted. "Again. Watch the shifts."

I sighed. Then started. I did it over and over. For her. For me. For some crazy reason I wasn't angry because I knew in my heart she was doing the right thing, so that I would become the best I could become.

"Listen," she said, "do you paint?"

I nodded.

"Paint the colors with sound."

I looked up at her husband's bold reds and blues and thought of the crashing sounds an orchestra can make.

"Do you write?"

"Poetry," I answered timidly.

"Excellent. We're storytellers in our own way through song. The instrument is our voice. Tell the story with your heart. Let the story sing, and unwind slowly. There's no need to rush it. Let the violin be your words. Now try again with a picture in your mind of the tale you alone will tell from the composer's piece."

When my mother picked me up, I was tired. Especially my arm and shoulder. Mrs. Lee smiled as my mother paid her. "See you next week," she said to me as the next student entered, looking prepared. "And practice! Four hours!"

As I walked toward the car my mother asked, "How did it go?"

"Okay," I said, hoping for "good" by next week. Always climbing higher.

"I need a coffee ice-cream soda," I said to my mother.

Roosevelt Field Mall is around the corner from Mrs. Lee's. We never go to malls. I mean never. Mom hates to shop. "They're overcrowded with people who feel they've died and gone to heaven," she says. But she loves me and could see I was desperate. We bumped into Barney Rosenthal and his mother eating cones outside of the main entrance.

When Barney saw me, he said, "So, Jason, how's it going?"

"Okay," I mumbled as I rubbed my neck.

"Did you hear about Mr. Carr?" he asked.

Barney's mother suddenly stopped talking to mine.

"What about him?" I asked.

"He might not come back."

"What do you mean?" I felt a knot in my stomach.

What about the chamber recitals he did every year? The auditions? I wanted to try out for the first time this year. Without him, would there be any recital? I was thinking about me, and not him. What was wrong?

"I've heard things, Lauren," Mrs. Rosenthal said smugly to my mother.

My mother looked at Mrs. Rosenthal. "What things?"

She glanced at her watch, avoiding my mother's question. "The PTA will be in touch with the parents. As president, I'll be on top of this situation. Don't worry."

14

"I wasn't," my mother said, looking very concerned.

What "situation"? I thought.

A fter the pledge, Mr. Carr announced over the PA system, "Welcome to a productive school year full of hard work and fun." Yes! He's back, I thought, when I heard his voice. So Barney's mother didn't know what she was talking about after all. A smile crossed Mrs. Jackson's face when she heard his voice. Mr. Carr called her "Mrs. J," and she called him "Mr. C." She told us he liked her idea of grouping our desks together in clusters instead of the usual straight, even rows. He felt it was "a creative approach."

During lunch, I headed for the Portable, a temporary building on the playground where we usually have group violin rehearsals. "Practicing on a lunch hour?" Barney shouted as I went past him, slamming his Spalding against the brick wall.

I didn't answer as I continued to walk, holding my violin. He went back to handball. From the large window inside the Portable I could see everything going on outside. Coach watched Caleb shoot hoops on the blacktop. I waved to them, and Caleb waved back. Some of the girls were practicing cheerleading routines. Tommy paused on the sidelines, tossing his baseball from hand to mitt. Then he elbowed Barney and they began imitating the girls, flapping their arms in the air like wings. Wendy was heading for a teacher's aide, probably to tell on them, when I started to play.

After a while, I turned around and saw Mr. Carr standing there. I jumped. "Sorry, I didn't hear you come in."

"You were involved," he said.

I paused, feeling shy. "It's okay, my being here? I got permission to practice. The aides are right outside."

He nodded approval. "Anyone who puts in this kind of time understands the commitment. Friends won't. Only those who are directly involved with you, or who do it themselves, will know the effort and the love that it takes each day." I wondered, how does he know all this? *He* understands. Then he stared at my violin. The wood grain shined in the sunlight. "I imagine your parents worked very hard to buy you such a nice violin. If you'd like to, you can keep it under the desk in my office." I thought of a year and a half of renting a bad one with steel strings and deep scratches.

Proudly, I told him, "I helped pay for the bow. I saved all my birthday gifts and money from my summer job. I walked Mrs. Peterson's fat, ugly dog when her arthritis acted up in the damp weather. Mrs. Peterson's. Not her dog's."

Mr. Carr howled. Then he said, "Try picking

the wild blackberries behind the school. You could sell them and use the money toward new strings! Strings are expensive."

"My father and I made a trip a few weeks ago into the city to buy strings cheaper. We went to a warehouse as large as an entire New York City block. The man who sold us the strings is very old. He sells Dominant and Pirastro strings to the Philharmonic. He sold the same kind to me." That gave me a thrill. Sort of the same thrill I saw on Tommy Wachowski's face while he shined the leather of his baseball mitt today before the big game at lunchtime. "Smell the neat's-foot oil," Tommy had said to me as he worked the dry surface until it was creamy. I knew how he felt as I inhaled the aroma of the cleaner. It reminded me of when I polished and buffed my violin.

The bell rang and recess was over. "See you inside," Mr. Carr said. "Remember, leave that instrument in my office, where it's safe." On his way out, he ran his finger across the velvet inside of my open case, and smiled.

Be careful with the strings, I reminded myself as I sat on the bench, rubbing them with alcohol, using an old white handkerchief I had borrowed from my father's dresser drawer. Grandma had given them to him after Grandpa died. Neatly folded and ironed into squares. Dad never used them, but I liked knowing it was one of Grandpa's handkerchiefs that I tucked under my chin before I played. I cleaned each string in one direction so it wouldn't get a burr. The white cloth became stained gray with sweat from my fingers, so I headed for the boys' bathroom in the main building to wash my hands. I met Tommy inside. He stepped away from the faucet and flicked some water in my face. I flicked some back, getting his T-shirt wet.

"Guess we could be in a wet T-shirt contest."

"You think you're real funny, Glass," Tommy said as both Barney and Caleb came out of stalls.

"I know I'm funny."

He moved closer. "I know you're a wuss."

My chest swelled with anger. My heart started thumping. The beat pounded loudly in my head. Do I say something? I dried my hands on a paper towel and turned toward Tommy. "What kind of a crack was that?"

"Anyone who plays violin when they could be playing baseball is a wimp. What's the matter? You think a precious finger might get squashed?" Tommy said as though he were talking to a little kid.

"Obviously," Caleb said, leaning toward Tommy, "you've gotten one too many IQ points knocked off in a game. It's amazing that with some people, whatever comes into their heads comes out of their mouths."

"Whether it makes sense or not," I piped in.

I shot a glance at Caleb. He smiled nervously. Tommy took a step in my direction. I could feel his breath on me when suddenly the door shot open.

18

"Everyone okay in here?" Mr. Carr asked.

There was dead silence. Tommy and I backed away from each other.

"Come on." Mr. Carr clapped his hands. "Time to get back to the classroom." He startled Barney, who turned quickly to go. Tommy followed, kicking an eraser he found down the hall like a hockey puck, carefree, forgetting his words. But I remembered.

Nothing could ruin my mood when I came home and saw Grandma Fanny sitting at the kitchen table having a cup of tea. I threw my backpack on a chair. "Darling, you look so skinny. What are you feeding him?" She turned to my mother.

Mom rolled her eyes. "Your son Hank's food."

"To think I slaved selling lingerie at Myrtle's on the Avenue so my only son could cook like his mother. *This* is a liberated world?" Grandma glanced up to the sky above.

Mom said that Dad's mother never got used to the fact that he became a chef instead of a doctor. My mother and father own "Comestibles," a small restaurant not far from where we live. *Comestible* means "food." Originally my father was going to go to medical school, but the summer before his senior year of college he went to the Culinary Institute of

America. Whenever he talked about the CIA, I thought he was a spy. Then I learned it wasn't the Central Intelligence Agency he was talking about.

"Grandma," I came to my father's defense, "Dad's a *great* cook."

"Maybe even better than his mother," Mom teased Grandma.

"A grown man *potchkehing* with pots." Grandma sighed.

"What's that funny word?" I asked.

"Playing." Mom laughed. "What David does with his fingerpaints."

"Fooling around, wasting time," Grandma explained to me. "Well, I admit he does work hard. It's not the kind of *nakhes* I had in mind."

"And that word?"

"Joy, pleasure, pride." Grandma hugged me.

"What I get from you when you play the violin." Mom smiled.

Now it was my turn to roll my eyes.

When I went to get a glass of milk, I saw a birthday card for Grandma on the refrigerator. David had made it in his typical crayon-and-paint style. He had also pasted and sprayed silver macaroni on the front.

"When David gets up from his nap, we'll leave for Grandma's party," Mom said, rubbing my back. Soon David trudged in, looking dopey.

Grandma showered David with kisses when he proudly handed her his card. It looked like it weighed a ton. "It's going on *my* refrigerator," Grandma said, "for all the neighbors to see when they come to visit. Now I can say I own an original David Glass."

"Or you could boil it for dinner if you run out of food," I said, thinking of all that macaroni hanging on the construction paper.

David punched me as Mom helped him put on his jacket. I gave him a light tap back. "Jason Glass, act your age." She gave me a look.

I *am,* I thought. I wasn't half-kidding anymore about wish number six, that David would disappear. Now it was a full-fledged wish.

We all left together in one car.

Grandma put her hand over her heart. "Don't drive so fast. I'd like to live to see seventy-one."

Mom bit her lower lip and slowed down to a snail's pace until we saw the green-and-white awning above the back entrance of the restaurant. We always go in through the kitchen, which makes me feel special because Luigi, the cook, looks up and yells, "The boys!" Luigi stuck his head out just as we got out of the car.

"Why did the CIA fire their chef?" I asked him.

"You tell me." He wiped his brow.

"Because the chef kept spilling the beans."

"That's a good one!" Luigi slapped my back.

As Luigi opened the door for Grandma, she smoothed the wrinkles from her dress and said to him, "Two men are in a restaurant."

21

"What kind?" David asked.

"It's unimportant," I said, feeling annoyed.

"It *is* important," David argued.

"A Chinese restaurant." I gritted my teeth.

"A Kosher restaurant," Grandma corrected me.

"See," David said triumphantly, "it really *was* important."

"Anyway," Grandma continued, "the first man asks for tea. 'Make sure the glass is clean,' he says to the waiter. When the waiter comes back, he says, 'Who gets the clean one?' "

David looked up at me. "I don't get it."

"Anything that isn't a knock-knock joke you don't get."

"Boys," Mom pleaded, "please, it's Grandma's birthday. Let's make this a nice evening. If not for her, at least do it for me."

"Very funny," David said to Grandma. He still didn't get the joke. She kissed him near his bangs anyway, and we went inside.

Grandma lifted the lid to a large pot.

"I bet it needs more salt," she said.

Dad looked at his mother and chuckled. "Hello, Ma. Happy Birthday." He gave her a peck on the cheek.

"Where's the salt?" she asked Luigi as if she didn't hear Dad.

"I don't cook with salt. There's basil in this sauce." He looked at my father helplessly. "Smell the herbs." Luigi sniffed in the aroma. "This special dish is in honor of you. Breast of Chicken à la Fanny."

"One taste, then." Grandma took a tiny sip from a wooden spoon and held it toward her mouth. "Not bad. Still could use a little salt."

Mom rolled her eyes again. She does that a lot when Grandma Fanny is around.

Dad seated us near a large round table in the corner so David could get up and down without bothering the customers. David sat in a chair between my mother and grandmother. Good. Peas and meatballs could bounce on someone other than me for a change. In the center of the table was a bouquet of red roses. "Grandpa used to buy me roses on special occasions." Grandma closed her eyes, took a deep breath as she smelled them, and smiled.

A new waiter came over. "My name is Enrico. tonight we have—"

"The Chicken Fanny," Grandma cut him off, finishing the sentence.

"I'll also have the Breast of Chicken à la Fanny." My mother turned to me. "Dad made it in a lemon Français sauce."

"Yum. Then I'll have it, too," I added.

I laughed when I saw the word FANNY up on the blackboard with the other dinner entrées. The blackboard is attached to a brick wall in the back near an open kitchen. Menus are never printed. Mom and Dad like to experiment with food that is available "in season" and looks good. Dad will go to the fruit and vegetable market at Hunts Point in the Bronx in the middle of the night to get the freshest ingredients. He'll buy bunches of kale and crates of grapefruit in the winter, and flats of strawberries in the summer. Whatever they don't use, the neighbors or shelters will be eating for a week. He wasn't popular the time he bought too many brussels sprouts. By the time I was nine, I was following in my father's footsteps. I could pick a ripe pineapple a mile away. Let's face it, it's hard to squeeze a pineapple. Dad taught me to use the old nozzle. Dad said that my sense of smell had become "impeccable."

David ordered his usual. "One meatball in pisgetti."

"Spaghetti," I said to the waiter. He nodded knowingly.

Dad didn't order. He rushed up and down to check the kitchen.

Before dessert, my father called me into the back. "I hope you don't mind. I asked your mother to sneak this in." He picked up my violin case. "Would you like to play 'Happy Birthday' for Grandma?"

"In front of everyone?"

"It's a piece of cake. No pun intended."

"That's easy for you to say." I peeked outside the kitchen. It was pretty crowded now. Glasses clinking. Waiters rushing. People talking. "I don't know." I shrugged.

"I don't want to push you."

"Da-a-d, I think you already did."

"For Grandma?" he begged.

Dad squeezed my shoulder as I tuned my violin. It had gotten out of tune from the steam swirling out of boiling pots throughout the kitchen. I walked up to the table where my family sat. I couldn't look at them. I could only play. I made the song sound fancier, vibrating my fingers on the strings with a lot of vibratos. Everyone applauded when I was done. A bead of sweat dripped down my back.

"Bravo!" shouted a man seated near the front window.

"Encore!" Grandma cried out. My face got hot, but I played a special klezmer piece for her. Klezmer is Jewish jazz, from Eastern Europe during the last century. It was music that Grandma's mother, Bubbe, had liked to hear. The music made Grandma's eyes tear. She blew her nose right at the end, which sounded like the final note. Everyone began to laugh because it was off-key. Grandma was laughing and crying at the same time. Only Grandma could do that.

"This has been a wonderful birthday, Sweetheart." Grandma kissed me. I turned red as a beet and wanted to crawl under the table. "Grandpa would have *kvehled*."

"Beaming with pride," Mom interpreted.

"He would have burst!" Dad added.

25

"That's too bad," David said sadly.

All the adults laughed. So did I, patting his head.

My father brought out the chocolate birthday cake that had made him famous: a tricolor mousse cake. White mousse. Chocolate mousse. And deep mocha on top of a bittersweet chocolate candy bar with raspberry squiggles. It caused one food critic to call him "the Jackson Pollock of Chocolate" because his squiggles looked like that painter's work.

Grandma Fanny was surrounded by all the waiters in the restaurant singing, "Happy Birthday to You." Everyone in the entire place joined in again. So did I, on the violin.

Later that night I ran into my parents' bedroom after brushing my teeth. Mom was reading in bed. Piled next to her tissue box were a bunch of novels, but as I leaned over to kiss her good night, I noticed the title of her book: *Living with AIDS, The Twentieth-Century Plague.* Who was sick? A neighbor? A friend? Someone in the *family*? I got scared. I never wanted to live without Mom or Dad. Even David the pest. Who would I tickle torture? I was too frightened to ask, because I didn't want any answers. But not knowing wasn't good, either. I hugged Mom tightly.

"You're squashing me." Mom sat up straight and gave me a big hug back.

"You're squashing *me*," I said. But I remained in her arms a few seconds longer than usual.

26

When I got into my own bed, I grabbed a piece of paper and a pencil so I could add to my wish list.

7) *I wish everyone in the world could have enough food. Especially egg rolls and knishes. And chicken soup. Except hot countries. They should have ice cream. Or lemon ices from the Ice King in Corona, Queens. Or maybe the vanilla with the chocolate chips. Yes, definitely that flavor. And toothpaste. A mushy pillow. And a warm bed.*

8) *I wish that Grandma will live to see me play in Carnegie Hall. That Grandpa hadn't died of cancer. I miss him. So does Dad. And Mom. And Grandma. David was still a baby. He never got to play checkers with Grandpa. Or plant morning glories. Or go with him to the aquarium to see starfish and baby belugas. There was so much left to see with Grandpa. Like me playing the violin. Grandpa never got to see that. I wish he had. And "kvheled."*

9) *I wish Mom and Dad and David will always be here. At least as long as I am.*

October

⁓✖⁓

The first Friday in October is traditionally "Pajama Day."

"As you know," Mr. Carr announced, "our graduation class is required to arrive at school tomorrow in pajamas. Anyone who doesn't come in the proper attire will be sent home or to the attendance office." Then he laughed over the loudspeaker.

"Why don't you wear some scanty silk number from the Victoria's Secret catalogue?" Tommy nudged Wendy.

Wendy's face flushed. "I'll have you know I'm wearing my flannel nightgown *over* a sweat suit."

"Sexy," he said, wiggling his eyebrows up and down.

"What are you wearing?" I asked Caleb at recess.

"Sweatpants and my 'Save the Rain Forest' T-shirt."

The next day, Tommy joked when he saw me wearing my dark green dinosaur slippers. "Looking good, Glass." When I walked down the hall they made a roaring sound—until the batteries gave out.

"You, too," I said sarcastically, eyeing him in his long underwear.

"How do you go to the bathroom in that getup?" Caleb asked.

"He's a camel. He holds it in all day," Wendy chimed in.

"If Clint Eastwood can wear them, I can," Tommy declared.

Usually, Tommy has to have the last word. This time it was Wendy.

"But you're no Clint Eastwood," she said.

When we paraded past Mr. Carr's office, he said to me, "Great footwear, Jason. Wish they came in my size." Mr. Carr was wearing a big bathrobe over pajamas with small yellow ducks on them, and a tie with M&M candies printed all over it.

"Nice tie, Mr. Carr," I said back.

He smiled, following our class into the gym, where assemblies are always held. The lower grades began to giggle and act silly when he went up to the microphone in the front near the stage. "What an upside-down day. This morning, we will have a bedtime story hour. As you can see, I'm prepared." He glanced down at his outfit. "There's a real treat in store from our wonderful kindergartners."

The lights lowered. Spotlights beamed across a large group of five-year-olds wearing claws and tails. Mr. Carr sat cross-legged on the corner of the stage. He wore furry brown bear claws! In his lap was an oversize copy of the book *Where the Wild Things Are*. The kindergartners acted out the words while he read them. It reminded me of second grade when Mr. Carr told us a fairy tale, and at the end he said, "At certain times, especially during a full moon, my toenails grow so long, they're the size of claws." I believed him and went home to make "Claw Counter-Potion Formula 70" to rid him of his "condition." I used petals from the rosebush in my backyard, leaf clippings, and orange juice, liquefying them in a blender. My father didn't appreciate it when he went to make one of his complicated sauces and found some red food coloring at the bottom of the blender. I had added it to make the potion look right. Dad cooled off when I told him it was for a good cause.

At the end of the assembly, after thunderous applause, Mr. Carr tapped the microphone and announced, "In November, there will be auditions for our spring Chamber Music Recital. As you know, everyone above grade four gets to play in a band or an orchestra. This is a little more special. We'll form a few select groups based on what Mr. Andrews, the music teacher up at the high school, hears. I'll put my two cents in, too." He chuckled. "So any of you who think you'd like to participate, sign up in the office. There will also be a solo performance."

My heart started racing at the idea of trying out.

Barney turned to me as I passed by. "I'm going for it."

"So am I," I said.

"Hey, just because I sit way back in the boon-docks with the second violins doesn't mean I shouldn't."

"Did you hear me say anything?" I asked.

"No. But I know what you're thinking," Barney yelled at me as Tommy pulled him away in his direction.

"Oh, you're psychic? You don't know what I'm thinking at all."

In my mind, only the word *solo* echoed.

That would be wish number ten.

After lunch, Caleb went home sick. I tele-phoned him the minute I got home from school. "We have a new student teacher, Miss Ryan. She's from a local college and is going to do her training in our classroom. And get this: She does taxidermy in her spare time!"

"Talk about weird." Caleb coughed into the receiver.

"Tommy couldn't contain himself. He asked her what she stuffed."

"Are you serious?" Caleb started coughing more from laughing.

"Mrs. Jackson gave him 'the look' as he said to her, 'How many times in my life am I going to meet someone who does this for a hobby?'"

Caleb blew his nose and lowered his voice, which was filled with curiosity. "So, did she tell him what she stuffed?"

"A parrot on a perch. And a guinea pig." I thought of Mr. Carr's cute guinea pig, Mr. Hobbs, whom he adopted when no one in our class could bring him home this past summer, and it gave me the shudders.

Caleb took it like the true medical student he wants to become: philosophically. "Everything has to die," he said to me.

I had no comeback for that.

Caleb broke the silence. "What did one taxidermist say to another after a big meal of venison?"

"Boy, do I feel stuffed?" I guessed. "Did you just make that up?"

"Yes. Can't pass anything over on you."

"Sounded like it." I moaned.

"Got another one. I guess you could say Mozart is *de*composing."

Before I hung up the phone, I added, in a perfect Arnold Schwarzenegger accent, "I'll be Bach."

Caleb groaned at the other end.

Weeks before the chamber music auditions, I practiced like crazy. I almost couldn't stand it anymore, wondering if all the work was worth it.

I had a dark red sore on the side of my chin where I placed my violin. Even Grandpa's white handkerchief didn't help, but I continued anyway. Mrs. Lee said, "Get used to it if you want to be a violinist when you grow up. Do your best. I won't say good luck. It's not luck, it's practice." But in my heart I felt a part of it was luck, too.

One night, during a long break, I laid my stamp collection out on my quilt and started arranging old stamps from Madagascar, Honduras, and Tasmania. When I heard my mother's footsteps coming down the hall, and then a knock at my bedroom door, I threw my pillow over the stamp album.

"Jason?"

I jumped up and immediately started playing again.

"What are you doing?" she asked, opening the door slightly.

"What do you think?" I said impatiently.

"You know what I think. I don't hear music. And when I do, it's pretty sloppy. You're slurring all the notes together. Slow down."

"Could you please leave?" I said.

"Could you please not use that tone?" She glanced down at a number of stray stamps on the floor. "You don't have to take lessons. You don't have to do this. It's your life. Don't do it for me or anyone. Do it for you."

"I know," I said.

"I mean it," she said.

"So do I," I said as I continued to play very, very slowly.

M r. Carr was out a lot or left school early, so he wasn't around to hear me practice in the Portable or during group violin lessons. But he made up for all his absences when he arranged a special field trip to the Museum of Modern Art to see the work of a painter named Matisse. The line of people to get in twisted around the entire block. "Let's sing songs," Mr. Carr shouted as he saw many of the kids getting bored, waiting. By the time we got inside, Mr. Carr even had strangers on line singing along with us.

The museum was jammed. I had to sneak in front of the adults to get a glimpse of a painting. Mr. Carr said, "When Matisse's art was first exhibited, critics called him 'a wild beast.' They hated his work and wouldn't let him show it. Look at these crowds now!"

"Like Tchaikovsky," I blurted out. "When his Violin Concerto in D Major was first performed in 1881, it bombed in a big way. Now every violinist in the entire world wants to play it." Listening to that piece is one of the things that makes me so happy, I feel as though I am bursting inside.

Mr. Carr looked at me and smiled broadly. "I guess they both saw the world in a different way. Their own way. Sometimes it's rough just being accepted."

As Halloween approached, David collected red and orange leaves and pressed them in a thick dictionary. I sprayed fake cobwebs on a spooky poster and carved pumpkins in school. There were Halloween safety skits in assembly about not going into strange houses, and checking apples for razor blades or unwrapped candy for poison. Miss Ryan tried to put the spirit back into things by wearing a pale pink leotard, wings, and holding a wand with a silver glittered star at the tip. Along with the kindergartners and first-graders in costumes, she trick-or-treated around the school, holding a shopping bag filled with goodies.

"What is she supposed to be?" Tommy blasted out in the art room.

"An elf?" I heard Barney say as he bent over a ceramic pot.

"Miss Ryan's a fairy. Like Mr. Carr," Tommy said in a high-pitched tone.

I looked at Caleb. He looked at me. What was that crack supposed to mean?

"You're a . . ." My voice trailed off. "I can't say

in public what I think you are. I don't know where you get these ideas from," I added.

"You talking to me?" Tommy looked up from a clay bust of himself that he was smoothing down with water.

"No, I'm talking to the fellow behind you." He turned around, and saw that behind him was a stack of sculptures. Caleb started to grin, and I had to hold myself back from grinning, too. But inside, I kept wondering why Tommy was saying these things about Mr. Carr. Was he jealous that Mr. Carr seemed to pay attention to me with the violin stuff? Mr. Carr was fair with everyone, so what was Tommy's problem? As for Barney, he goes along with anything Tommy says. He doesn't have a brain of his own.

Tommy leaned over and pressed his thumb into a piece of clay I had formed into a long snake-like rope. I glared at him and began to roll it between my fingers again. Without saying a word to each other, Caleb and I figured out it was best to leave it alone. Tommy is a jerk. And that was that.

"You're chicken," Tommy tried to taunt me.

"I'm not going to get into a fight with you. If you want to think I'm a chicken, think I'm a chicken. I know I'm not. I know what I am."

"And what's that?"

"Brave. It takes more courage to be different than the same."

Tchaikovsky knew it. So did Matisse. And Mr. Carr, and me.

November

∞

The morning of the audition, I had to leave class early to go to the high school. On my way out, Miss Ryan whispered, "Break a string."

"What did she say?" Barney asked, racing toward the school van waiting in the parking lot, his violin case flapping against his leg.

"Nothing much." I slinked into a backseat and filled the space next to me with my violin case.

Barney sat across the aisle from me, beside Brandon, who was trying out with his flute. They were friends, even though Brandon was a fifth-grader. We were all in the same Hebrew school car pool together. The van was packed with other fifth- and sixth-graders and their instruments by the time we left. I turned away and stared out the window, needing quiet. The crossing guard was walking a few latecomers across the street to the school entrance. The only time I had been late was in fifth grade, the morning after the Long Island String

37

Festival. My parents had taken me out to celebrate for ice cream afterward. I was the second chair in the first violin section for the whole county. But I wanted more. I wanted first chair.

Classes were changing as we entered the high school and headed for the large music room. Everyone seemed tall like my father. It made me feel young and alone, until I found my way to Room 101 and saw Mr. Carr leaning over a piano bench, flipping through some music.

"Sit here." He waved and motioned for me to come over.

I made my way toward the old upright piano, past groups of kids from other schools who were gathered around it, tuning up. A girl from the high school moved a music stand out of my way. When she turned around, I realized it was Alexandra Wheaton, a senior. Her parents are members of our synagogue. "Thanks," I said, remembering that she had gotten a scholarship to the Aspen Music Festival this past summer. She had started playing when she was three years old at a Suzuki School and had learned to play by ear, without reading music, probably along with a group of thirty other three-year-olds. At that age, my interests were playing with blocks and plastic farmyard animals on our living-room rug.

She plucked a few strings and warmed up with some arpeggios.

"Nice sound," I said.

"You think so?" She adjusted the shoulder rest. "This is my school violin. My good one is at home."

"Oh." I fidgeted with my handkerchief. Why hadn't she brought it to the audition? Maybe this was no big deal for her? It was to me.

Mr. Andrews tapped a pedestal with a raised baton. "People, let's begin, or else we'll be here all day. Most of you know my colleague, Mr. Carr." He pointed in his direction. Mr. Carr's hand trembled as he stood up and held on to the piano. I wondered why. "After each name is called, we'll both listen for about five minutes, tops. Any questions?"

"When are the solo tryouts?" a girl off to the side asked.

"Before the spring recital, we'll announce it. So let's have some quiet in here right now. Sherman Elementary is first."

Everyone's performance melted off into the distance. Even Barney's. And Brandon's. Then I heard my name. "Next, Jason Glass."

"That's me," I said. My stomach was in knots.

I made a mistake. My heart sank. One note wrong. *Keep going. Recapture the sonata. Stronger. Softer here. Don't let up. Do it!*

"Let's break," Mr. Carr said to Mr. Andrews, looking pale.

Was I *that* bad?

He seemed winded and tired. "Good job, Jason."

"Thanks," I said, putting my violin back in its case.

There was a part of me that wanted to ask him, do you think I'll be placed in a group? But when I turned around, he was gone.

As I was waiting for the others to finish, an older boy sat down, holding a violin. "He's great, isn't he?" he said to me.

"Who?" I asked, thinking he meant one of the players.

"Mr. Carr. He was my principal years ago. He helped me with my English when I came over here from China. For an entire week after I arrived, he had the whole school doing tai chi each morning on the playground field. He blasted Chinese music over the loudspeaker while I taught these movements along with my grand-parents. He made me and them feel important. He's a real nice guy."

"He sure is," I said.

"Well, good luck. See you around," he said.

Hope so, I thought. "See you."

When I got back to school, the first thing I saw was Caleb's face. "How did you do?" he asked.

I shrugged. "I don't know."

"You always say that, and you do okay."

"Mr. Carr had to leave the tryouts, so I don't know. He looked pretty sick."

"The flu's going around. Miss Ryan left. She vomited."

"Near Tommy's or Barney's desk?" I asked gleefully, hoping.

"Jason," Caleb said, "she made it to the bathroom."

"I hope I don't get it," I said.

"Me neither," Caleb added.

The next day, Mrs. Jackson handed a note to me, and another to Barney.

Dear Jason,
I enjoyed hearing you play yesterday. Sorry I had to leave so abruptly. If I'm not in school tomorrow, I just wanted to let you know that you will be in a quartet. Definite groups will be formed in January.

Congratulations!
Mr. Evan Carr

P.S. Keep up the good work!

I turned around to glance at Barney. He looked disappointed.

He walked by my desk, crumpled his note, and tossed it into the wastebasket. "Guess you made it," he said, seeing how happy I was.

I didn't answer, although there was a part of me that wanted to rub it in. "You'll still be in the spring concert," I said to him.

"Yeah." He shrugged. "I didn't care anyway."

"Yeah, sure."

Mrs. Jackson cleared her throat. "Mr. Carr will be out for a few days, but he asked the teachers to remind all of you that Thanksgiving is coming up soon. He'd like our school to do a food drive for the homeless. Any extra canned goods, boxes of rice, spaghetti, that you can spare would be nice."

"What about frozen stuff? Like pizza?" Tommy joked.

Mrs. Jackson just stood there shaking her head back and forth.

Every day before Thanksgiving, we made a food count.

"There's so much tuna here," Tommy said as he sorted through the pile in the cartons, "the people we donate this stuff to will sprout gills and fins."

"My mother's going to send in a turkey," Wendy said.

"Turkey in a can?" Tommy asked.

"No, a real one. We'll bring it to the shelter."

Tommy knelt down in front of her on his knees with his hands cupped together, begging. "Please sir, I want some more," he said with a British Cockney accent like in the musical *Oliver*. Last year in the school play, he had the part of Oliver, one of the boys in the orphanage, because he has a good singing voice. He should have played Fagin, the evil leader of the young pickpockets and thieves. Mr. Carr played Fagin. He was definitely miscast. Mr. Carr could never be that mean. My mother said that *her* old principal would have qualified for the part. He used to pin "bad" students to the wall a foot off the ground, which scared her so much in first grade, she once peed in her underpants during lunchtime.

"What did you bring in?" Wendy cross-examined him.

Tommy dug his hands deep into his ripped pockets. "Stuff."

"Like what?" she drilled him.

"I don't remember, just stuff."

I glanced over at a hole near the elbow of his shirt. Buttons were missing near his frayed collar. "I saw him put something in," I offered, coming to his defense, without knowing exactly why.

Tommy looked surprised, almost as surprised as I was.

Our school came in first in the district, hitting the 3,000 mark of canned goods. Mr. Carr was back by then and he said, on one of the days he was in school, "Let's have a big party the day before Thanksgiving recess! Everyone will bring in a dish from their heritage. It will be an international luncheon of all the nationalities in Sherman Elementary."

"Oh, a potluck dinner!" Wendy squealed.

"Oh, I love those!" Tommy mimicked in a high voice.

"We could do a cookbook of all the recipes," I said.

"What a great idea." Wendy smiled at me.

"Violin, cooking. Hey, Glass, do you do basket making in your spare time?" Tommy rested his head on his hand. "I'm making my famous Rice Krispies bars. Pour in one box of cereal. Melt one bag of marshmallows."

Barney said, "I'll help you. I'll throw in chocolate chips."

"What country is that from?" Wendy asked. "Moron?"

Caleb and I couldn't help laughing, even though it was mean.

The day of the luncheon, my mother drove me to school. I headed straight for the cafeteria to drop off my contribution: matzoh-ball soup. My mother admitted as we were rolling the matzoh meal, "The secret to making the balls extra fluffy is a spritz of seltzer. Just a touch."

"Grandma Fanny's?" I asked.

"Grandma Fanny's," she said. "Maybe I shouldn't reveal this fact to anyone, but if it wipes out bowling balls in chicken soup, I feel that I will have added to the well-being of mankind. Womankind, too."

I was behind Caleb on line as we browsed the long tables, choosing unfamiliar foods. Mrs. Jackson brought in a delicious sweet potato pie, and Miss Ryan, a large crock of Irish lamb stew.

When Tommy saw sushi, he squirmed. "What's that?"

"Raw fish and pickled vegetables," Chisato said.

"I don't like my things still alive."

"Oh, Tommy," she insisted, "try it. In Japan, we love it."

"Is that a tentacle?" he asked hesitantly, poking the food with a plastic fork.

"Octopus," she said.

"It tastes like chicken," Caleb and I said together.

"Sure it does." Tommy looked doubtful as he popped one in his mouth and held it there without swallowing. When Chisato wasn't looking, he spit it into a napkin. At least he didn't do that in front of her.

"I should have brought in sweetbreads," I said to Caleb.

"A true delicacy," Caleb said to me like an English butler.

"I love sweets. And bread," Tommy said.

"It's made from the pancreas or thymus of a calf," Caleb said.

Tommy paled and looked a little nauseous. "Thanks for sharing that with me, Harmon," he said, balancing his paper plate.

"I couldn't resist," I whispered to Caleb.

Caleb baked Irish soda bread, scones, and Scotch-bread cookies for dessert. They were all a bit on the dry side. I didn't want to hurt his feelings, so I slurped them down with my chicken soup as we sat down to eat near Mrs. Jackson at our class table. Some teachers and staff were lined up at a dais in the front with Mr. Carr in the center. Everyone was busy talking and eating, except Mr. Carr, who wasn't eating at all. It was the first time I noticed how thin he had become. I whispered in Caleb's ear, "That flu must have hit him really hard."

The letter came during Thanksgiving recess. Caleb and I were outside riding bikes. As the sun went down, we went inside for some hot chocolate, and I noticed the school stationery.

"What's this?" I picked the letter up from the countertop.

My mother looked distracted, circling Big Boy tomatoes in a seed catalog. "Oh, it's from the superintendent's office."

I read aloud to Caleb. "'Dear Parents and Students: Mr. Evan Carr went down to Virginia to visit his family for a few weeks to recuperate from an illness. We'll keep everyone posted. Have a nice vacation. Dr. Justin Healy, Superintendent of Schools.'"

"What kind of illness?" I asked my mother. "A bad strain of the flu? I thought he was getting better. He was back in school this week. So what is it? A virus? Pneumonia?"

"Or some rare disease? Is it catching?" Caleb probed further.

"Someone who dissects bugs and wants to be a microbiologist isn't going to take this sitting down, are they?" my mother poked fun at Caleb.

Caleb nodded in agreement. "Remember the time Ms. Levy looked like she'd been chugging one too many milk shakes, and we finally found out she was going to have a baby?"

"Yeah," I said, wondering where he was heading.

"Then Barney Rosenthal got this thing called 'the fifth disease' and no one knew what the other four were. Ms. Levy decided she'd better stay home if she wanted to have a baby that looked as though it didn't come from Mars?"

I nodded.

"Didn't Mr. Carr go on a safari in Africa a year ago? Do you know how many undiscovered viruses there are in the rain forests?" Caleb said.

"He'll be okay," I said, wiping whipped cream from my upper lip. "He keeps the health food store in business. He puts wheat germ on his yogurt."

"What kind of germ?" Caleb asked.

My mother tousled my hair. I looked up at her over my mug of hot chocolate. "You worry too much," she whispered in my ear.

"Okay," I said in resignation.

Caleb called me before we went to sleep. "I researched 'the fifth disease.' It's highly contagious. The telltale symptoms are a slapped-face appearance and a red rash on the arms and legs in the pattern of a lace curtain. The other four diseases are measles; German measles, also known as rubella; mumps; and chicken pox."

"Now I can sleep comfortably, Dr. Harmon."

"Glad to be of service," he teased back and hung up.

After vacation, when I walked up the front steps to the redbrick school building, I felt strange not seeing Mr. Carr. Caleb was carrying one of the unfinished charts he had done for our science project. A rubber band popped and I ran over to help him. "You okay?" I asked.

"I'm okay." As he bent down and fumbled to roll up the oaktag, he grabbed my arm and nodded silently. Somehow I felt we would always be best friends.

A new voice came over the PA system when we settled in the classroom. "Hello, boys and girls. My name is Ms. Mosely. I will be the acting principal until Mr. Carr feels well enough to return."

"That's a good sign, 'acting' principal," Wendy whispered.

Tommy shouted out, "What's she acting for? Why doesn't she get real?" Then he added, "Hey, when's Mr. C. coming back?"

Mrs. Jackson tapped her toe. "No one's certain. Hopefully, soon." She pressed her dark brown lips together and sighed. "I thought it would be nice for each of you to write and illustrate a poem to send to Mr. Carr while he's away, so he feels we're still with him."

Wendy Wein's hand shot up. "We could make a scrapbook."

"Great," Tommy smirked, "just what I wanted to do."

"And I could help sew it," Miss Ryan added.

"I bet she'd be good at that," Tommy muttered.

I thought the whole idea was neat. A bound book.

"Can we write about anything?" I asked.

"Anything." Mrs. Jackson smiled.

So I wrote about a painting I liked at the Matisse exhibition. I remembered Mr. Carr liked it, too, and we stayed in front of it and stared after everyone had moved on to the next one.

FRENCH WINDOW AT NICE (1919)

Alone in terror
Stuck in two dimensions
She tries breaking through.
Trapped in an alcove.
Nowhere to go. Out.
One escape. No way through.
Everything excels and moves.
She cannot make din.
Feet nailed to the floor.
Small, in such a large world.

At the end of the day, Ms. Mosely announced the bus schedule. "Bus A-1, please line up." Then she said as an afterthought, "Oh, yes, Mr. Carr telephoned. He sends all of you his greetings."

"Mr. Carr sends you his greetings," Tommy repeated. "That's it? Period? Mr. C.'s never been short on words. Something's up."

For the first time, I agreed with Tommy.

December

❦

Sunday morning, a week after Thanksgiving recess, my father drove the car pool to Hebrew school. Caleb was going to Bible class at his church, so we agreed to meet after we were both through. Dad whistled along with the radio as we headed for Wendy Weins's house. He paused at a stop sign and looked at me. "Jason, are you worried about something?"

"Not really," I lied, thinking, tomorrow's Monday: school. I like school, but I also like being away from it, and lately, I was getting sick of Tommy's teasing. I could handle him, but who needed it? I also wondered what would happen to the chamber groups and practice with Mr. Carr away.

Dad beeped the car horn as we entered Wendy's driveway. He rubbed his hand back and forth on my shoulder. "Jas, if there's anything wrong, I'm here. Always remember that." His blue-gray eyes twinkled.

Wendy walked down the slate path toward our car and slid into the backseat. "Hi, Mr. Glass," she said politely.

"Next Stop, Mr. Rosenthal." Dad did his best bus driver voice.

Barney took his time getting into the car as he munched on a bag of peanuts. The car began to smell like the circus so I opened my window. Every week, he came into the car eating something. Chips. Cookies. Crackers. Anything that made crumbs.

"Did you finish your report on photosynthesis?" he asked.

Wendy said "yes" as I said "no."

"Caleb and I are finishing up the rest this afternoon."

"You're supposed to work independently," Barney informed us.

"Mrs. Jackson told us that we could draw charts. Together."

"Artwork isn't research," Barney added between crunches.

I gritted my teeth. "*Scientific* charts."

Dad made the last stop at Brandon Greenberg's house. As Barney shifted over when Brandon got inside the car, I imagined Brandon sitting on stray peanuts, and I was glad I was in the front next to my father.

"Hi," Brandon said cheerfully.

"Hi," we all said in unison.

"Heard you made the cut for the chamber recital," he said. I nodded. Barney stopped munching. "I didn't. Maybe I'll try again next year. If they even have it," Brandon continued. "Did you hear that Mr. Carr might never be coming back?"

"Where did you hear that?" I asked, trying not to sound panicked.

"My mother heard it from your mother." Brandon looked at Barney.

I twisted around in my seat belt. "Is that true?"

Barney funneled the last bit of peanuts into his mouth and punched the small bag, making a loud pop. As my father edged up the circular driveway to let us off, Barney said, "Yeah, it's true."

"Last stop, Temple Beth Shalom," my father said, waiting for us to exit. "Learn a lot." He waved good-bye to me.

Barney was the last one out of the car and he nearly tumbled onto Wendy when she stopped short. "The letter said he's recuperating. Why's he leaving?" Her frown changed to a broad grin as Rabbi Schwartz greeted us.

"What do I look like, the PTA president?" Barney said as he plopped a silk yarmulke on his head, one that was left over from his sister's Bat Mitzvah service a month ago.

"No," said Wendy, "you resemble her son."

My mind wandered while Miss Bloom read us Bible stories. All I could think about was Mr. Carr not returning. He *had* to see me in the Chamber

Music Recital. And what about the auditions for the solo?

When I blinked, the morning was over.

Mrs. Rosenthal carpooled home. I climbed in her silver station wagon behind Barney. "Buckle up," she ordered. Brandon looked sheepishly at me as he fastened his seat belt. Mrs. Rosenthal checked her rearview mirror, braked, and waited until I finished doing mine. At the sound of the metal click, she moved toward the exit, down the winding hill.

"Mommy," Barney said.

Mommy? I thought.

"Did you tell Brandon's mother that Mr. Carr isn't going to be our principal anymore?"

Mrs. Rosenthal tightened her lips into a straight line.

Barney turned around triumphantly to the three of us in the backseat. "You see, I told you so."

"Don't spread rumors," Wendy whispered. "Gossip is mean."

"A rumor is something that isn't so; this is," Barney insisted.

"A rumor is an unconfirmed story in circulation," Mrs. Rosenthal said. "He's too weak to resume his normal schedule."

Mrs. Rosenthal sounded so angry, I couldn't help saying, "Mr. Carr can't help it if he's sick."

"Hmmph," she grumbled, "but he *could* have."

Wendy shrugged and looked at me, confused. "What's that supposed to mean?" she asked softly.

"I can't believe it," Brandon said. "He's been our principal since kindergarten."

"Believe it," Barney said. "He's history."

The words "since kindergarten" remained. Mrs. Jackson was okay. So was Miss Ryan. But would a new principal understand me like Mr. Carr? Would that person let me practice during lunchtime in the Portable? And let me keep my violin in their office? And root for me during solo tryouts?

When I got home, my father glanced up. He was poring over some recipe books while David was making spaghetti strands out of pasty-white Play-Doh. Big brown globs surrounded them.

"What are those?" I pointed.

"Meatballs," he said proudly.

"I should have known. Your favorite. They look gross."

"They look scrumptious." Dad gave me his "be-quiet-if-you-want-to-live" look. "How did your morning go?"

"Okay." I dumped my Hebrew books on the countertop.

"Just okay?"

"Just okay," I repeated, feeling impatient.

"Caleb called. He wanted to know if you could come over for lunch. You can go as long as you wind it up by five. We're having dinner together for a change," Dad said, turning to a page on yeast breads.

"What's the occasion?" I questioned.

"Nothing. I know it seems strange that two parents who are constantly wrapped up with food rarely eat together, but that's the way it is. I can't help it." He sighed in a defeated way. I put my arms around my father's waist. "I needed that," he said.

"Me, too," I said back.

"Family hug," yelled David, dashing out of his chair. I ducked away from his moist fingers. He held his small smeared hands in the air. "Please, I won't get you dirty. I promise. Pretty please," he coaxed.

"Oh, okay," I groaned as I let him squash in between Dad and me.

My father looked down at me and smiled, mouthing, "Thanks."

I pulled away to call Caleb as soon as David began to squirm. David looked disappointed. He could have gone on like this until I could no longer breathe. Mom always called him "the PC" in the family, "the Professional Cuddler."

"It's me," I said into the receiver when I heard Caleb's voice.

"Can you come over now?" he asked eagerly.

My father gave me a lift. Caleb waved when he saw me. A lot of people think we are brothers, sometimes even twins, because we both have long, reddish-brown hair and freckles. Except he always has a smile on his face. I just smile if I feel like it, and there are times I don't. Right now, I didn't.

"Do you want to build a fort inside?" he asked

as I made my way toward him through the slush.

"Sure." I followed him around the side of his house to the back porch, where we left our snow boots. Our old jars were filled with ice. We went in through the kitchen, passing our plant project in the greenhouse window. Lima beans and avocado pits were growing under artificial and natural light. We kept track of their growth on a chart next to the windowsill.

"Hi, Jason." Caleb's mother paused from marking papers.

"Hello, Mrs. Harmon," I answered.

"I'm hungry," Caleb said.

My stomach grumbled as I noticed the pizza box on the counter.

"I'll nuke some slices," he said.

"Just let me take this pile away before you both get sauce all over it. I don't think my students will appreciate greasy biology exams handed back to them on Monday."

Mrs. Harmon shuffled sheets of paper into one neat stack. As she placed the tests in the dining room, several school notices scattered onto the table. One was from the Parents Council Board. Another was sent to all the members of the PTA committee. Caleb's mom is also the class mother, along with Mr. Thomas Wachowski, Sr., Tommy's father, who runs a plumbing business out of a trailer next to his house. On the side of his truck is a cartoon picture of a pipe dreaming of a new bathroom. A bubble rises out of the top and has a caption that says PIPE DREAMS. We had never heard of a class father. Neither had Tommy's father until Mrs. Jackson asked him. "Yeah, why not? I'll do it for the kid," he said, meaning Tommy.

Tommy's mother died less than a year ago of leukemia. Everyone in town wonders if it was because their house is near the landfill. I can't imagine my mother never hugging me again or not tucking the blankets close to my body at night and giving me a butterfly kiss with her eyelashes on my cheek.

When Caleb's mother went into the dining room, I whispered, "I heard in carpool this morning that Mr. Carr might not be coming back to school. What do you think is the matter?"

"My mother was talking on the phone, and all I heard were her words 'they say he's getting emaciated day by day, but his spirits are the best they could be, considering.'"

"Considering what?" I looked at Caleb.

"Forget it. Come on, let's build a tent out of blankets after lunch. We'll play Clue or Monopoly inside. Or poker."

Caleb and I built a tent between his bed and desk out of his father's moth-eaten woolen army blanket and Caleb's old patchwork quilt from when he was a baby. We sat inside, moving Colonel Mustard and Professor Peacock around the board from the library to the conservatory, until Caleb made an accusation, breaking the silence. "Miss

Scarlet with a wrench in the billiard room." The game went fast since it is next to impossible to play Clue with two people. Next, we played hearts.

"It's getting stuffy in here," I said, feeling the lack of air.

We ripped apart the tent. A sudden gush of cool air made me dizzy. I went through the motions of lettering our science report with Magic Markers, doing the diagrams of leaf structures on oaktag, but there was this awful nagging tug inside, and I knew Caleb felt it, too, because he wasn't smiling. He almost always smiles. My eyes met his.

"There's something wrong with Mr. Carr, right?"

Caleb drew in a deep, deep breath. "I think he's got AIDS."

"Is everything all right?" my father asked when I slid into the front seat next to him. "Did you and Caleb have a fight?" I felt hot tears coming. Burning. I rubbed my eyes, trying to stop them.

"Remember today, earlier, in the car pool, all that conversation about our principal not coming back?"

"Sort of. I wasn't paying much attention," Dad said, lowering the radio. He had an old tape of The Doors on. His music.

"It seems like it's true. Mr. Carr might have"— I tried to clear the lump in my throat—"AIDS. Caleb said so."

My father pulled the car over and stopped in a wooded area. When he shut the radio off, there was a sudden hushed quietness. He put his large arms around me. His hair smelled of peppermint shampoo. His familiar odor made me feel safe.

"Jason, Jason, Jason," he kept repeating, hugging me tighter.

"Dad," I looked up at him, "it's like when we found out that Grandpa was going to die and there was nothing anyone could do to save him." My father nodded. "I knew I'd never hear that dumb laugh of his that made everyone who heard it laugh along with him. In the same way, almost every day of my life since I've been little, I've seen Mr. Carr's face, and it's so full of happiness."

"It's a nice way to begin each day," my father said.

"He's the first person who told me that I was good at the violin. I didn't know what I was doing. I was just playing. If he hadn't encouraged me, I might not be taking lessons now. You know, he lets me keep my violin in his office when I'm not using it. And he locks the door when he leaves. You didn't know that, did you?"

I watched my father rub the bristles of his unshaven face. His brow tightened, forming deep lines in his forehead. "Mr. Carr is a very sweet man. Nothing can ever change that. And no one. No matter what anyone says or tells you. It's the person inside that comes out through the little things they do and don't do. You can't always listen to what people say. It's what they *do* in life. Their actions really reveal who they are. And he has supported your music. I've learned that talk is cheap."

"When did you learn that?" I asked.

Dad sighed. "Oh, it wasn't any specific time. Over and over it becomes evident as you live a life. I guess one thing I remember is when my father was dying and how everyone said they would help. They couldn't and didn't. People get involved in their own everyday lives. You learn to depend on yourself, which really isn't such a bad thing. It allows you to grow. And that's good."

"But I depend on Caleb," I said. "When my newt was lost, Caleb spent a whole day searching for Newton with me and found him in the little dish of water that you suspended from the grill in front of the heating vent. Caleb said it was like Newton was visiting a steam bath."

"Then you have found a true friend. That makes me feel good."

"I've found more than one friend. In a way, Mr. Carr has become like a friend, too, because he cares."

I thought of what I wrote in my third-grade journal. I found it over the weekend and ripped out the page to save:

A good friend will not be bossy (like Tommy W.).
A good friend will play with you and be with you
    (like Caleb H.).

A good friend will not run away from you.
They will run to you.

When Mrs. Cohen, my teacher, hung up in the hall what we had written, Mr. Carr scrawled at the bottom, "These certainly are fine qualities for a friend to have. I think you would be a good friend."

Dad messed up my bangs. "You know what?"

"What?"

"You're very lovable." He hugged me tightly.

"I know."

"You know?"

"Yeah. Mom tells me all the time."

Dad gave me a playful punch in the arm.

"Hey, watch out," I shouted, "that's my bowing arm."

"Kiddo, the other one is. That's the one that holds the violin."

"Same difference."

Before Dad turned the key in the ignition and drove us home, he said, "You know you're getting older when your son has some wisdom, too."

Our house was filled with cooking smells. Not like Grandma's. Dad says her house smells like she uses boiled chicken air freshener. You can sniff the aroma of her apartment out in the hall before you even enter. Stuffed derma, brisket, and meatloaf are Grandma's three basic food groups.

My mother glanced up from the open oven,

basting a small turkey, as we came in. "How're my boys doing?"

Dad looked at me. "Jason's very upset."

She pushed the rack back inside, put the wooden spoon and glass baster down, and then faced me wearing two flowered oven mitts. "About what?"

"It seems"—Dad motioned for Mom to sit down as he pulled out a chair—"that Jason found out today Mr. Carr isn't coming back."

Mom glanced at me and then back at Dad. She swept her hair off to the side and blotted herself with the dishtowel that hung through a loop on her jeans. Mom looked straight at me, said nothing, and then pulled me toward her. I could feel her heart thumping against mine.

"Why didn't you just tell me?" I asked.

"Because I wasn't sure, and I know how much you like Mr. Carr. Some people say he has cancer. Maybe hepatitis B, or the HIV virus that causes AIDS. No one is sure. The school system has told us just what you saw. The letter. That's all."

"Really, that's all?"

"Really," she said. "I didn't want to worry you. I love you very much. I'm sorry for all the children in the school, but I'm most sorry for Mr. Carr. You're graduating, moving on."

I rubbed my eyes. "Mom, you're not making me feel any better."

"I don't know if I can. Adults can't always fix things."

Dad put his hand on my shoulder. "Sometimes we have to learn to accept what is. And go on. That's the only way to survive."

I lowered my head. "It's hard." I paused. "How did Mr. Carr get AIDS? Did he have a transfusion that time he had his tonsils out?" I asked.

"I don't know," Mom said.

"He didn't take drugs," I added, thinking of his campaign to make all the schools a "drug-free zone." "Is he gay?" I asked.

"I think so," my mother answered.

"Oh," I said, letting that settle in a minute. I shrugged. "I just want him to be okay."

David came in, dragging a noisy bumblebee toy on a long string. It made a buzzing sound as he scooted by. "Is dinner ready?"

"Soon," Mom said, picking him up in her arms and kissing his chubby red cheeks.

"You're squishing me, Mommy!" David squirmed from her grasp.

"No, I'm holding on," she whispered.

Dad kissed the tops of their heads, and then mine.

David and I set the table. As I put away my photosynthesis chart explaining chlorophyll, and my bean seeds in the peat pots with the wooden markers saying NO SUNLIGHT and SUNLIGHT, I read to the end where we stated: "In the absence of light, leaves become smaller, plant growth diminishes, and as soon as the plant uses up its stored food, it dies."

I decided I needed to write to Mr. Carr.

After dinner, the light from the street lamppost reflected leaflike patterns across my desk. I sat, connecting the freckles on my arm with my finger as though they were constellations, and thought about the day, how it had begun like any other ordinary day. Then I heard the news. Just like the time with Grandpa Sy. The day changed, and it wasn't like any other. I wished I could turn the clock back, wake up, and it would evolve in a different way, but it couldn't. It didn't. Because that's the way things go. Out of control. Sometimes it is exciting, like the time there was a hailstorm in the middle of July and pellets came down on the roof the size of golf balls. Other times, it is scary, like today.

I fished out a piece of lined paper from my loose-leaf notebook. When my eyes adjusted to the blackness of my room, I found the switch to my lamp. The lamp looks like a very large pencil, almost three feet high. It was from my grandfather's office. Wherever I go, I'll take that lamp with me, and his glass paperweight with marbleized swirls inside. I wrote at the top: *Dear Mr. Carr.* What could I say? I'm sorry. People told my father at Grandpa's funeral how sorry they were, but they made pigs of themselves at the luncheon afterward. Dad's sisters took home plastic tubs of leftover potato salad and coleslaw. Each aunt grabbed a fruit basket. Even Grandma Fanny talked about other things. Empty things that didn't count: like the weather, who sent their regards, and some third cousin who just had a baby. Sorry didn't seem to be enough. Maybe people said it when they didn't know the person. What he thought, what he felt inside.

As a little kid I was never big on make-believe. In first grade, I wished there was a Santa Claus who would leave Jewish children presents. Rabbi Schwartz would have a coronary if he knew. Someone who would park his sleigh on my roof, make his way inside our house, even without a chimney. I wished for a plush stuffed dog. A dalmation with black spots. In the middle of the night when I got up to get a drink of water, I saw my father dragging an enormous carton in the living room. He put it in front of the window where the menorah stood facing a street lined with twinkling Christmas lights. Spotty slept with me for two years. His large glass eyes were always there to listen to my secrets, until I pushed him out of my bed and into a closet as I grew up.

Make-believe ended when I was eight. Grandpa became too weak to walk like he used to. His face constantly showed pain. His skin varied from a pale yellow to a washed-out gray. He no longer smiled or told jokes. Instead, he winced or held his side suddenly. The endless afternoons of playing Chinese checkers, arguing over who got Boardwalk, and whether or not to build hotels on

St. James Place were over and replaced by the family's conversation of what to do about Grandpa. When Grandma was around his illness was ignored as if he were fine.

There was a part of me that wanted to imagine make-believe was real. It kind of began again when I was nine and discovered the magical sound that strings could make when my fingers touched them, and the beautiful music I heard by great musicians. Music that didn't feel as though it came from this earth. I dreamed of standing in a spotlight alone, playing. It was Mr. Carr who fed those dreams, easing me along. He and I both knew that. How could I tell him this now? I left the page blank. Then I started at the only place I could, at the beginning.

> *Dear Mr. Carr,*
>
> *You started my dreams and nurtured them. Caleb Harmon and I are doing a science project on photosynthesis. In a way, I was your lima bean seed, your plant. I am growing in the light you provided. I'm sorry you are sick. I hope you return. I'm going to miss you if you don't.*
>
> *Sincerely yours,*
>
> *Jason Glass*

Gee, I thought to myself, I said the one thing I didn't want to say, that I was sorry.

Caleb said, "On Friday, Mr. Carr's resignation is final."

"You're sure?" I asked as we headed for the school bus.

"My mother heard. You know she's class mother," he said.

I kicked a pebble on the ground. There was nothing to say.

That evening, my mother announced, "I'm going to a PTA meeting."

"You never go," I said.

"Jason, I'm either working or taking care of David."

"So how come you're going tonight?"

"Tonight will determine Mr. Carr's future."

"Can I come?" I asked.

"Parent-Teacher meeting," Mom said. *"Not students."*

"Okay, I get the picture," I said, disappointed, as she walked to the front hall closet to put on her winter coat.

"Bye!" she yelled to Grandma and David, who were busy playing checkers.

"Bye!" I shouted back and began tuning my violin.

"Don't rush home," Grandma said as she sat on the living-room floor and jumped one of David's red plastic checkers.

"Let's play a different game," David pouted.

Then he changed his mind after Grandma let him get two of her black pieces.

My mother stuck her head in the room. "Don't forget to brush your teeth." When she swung around, her dangling silver earrings jingled like the tiny bell in Sniffles's ball.

Grandma, David, and I played a few rounds of Go Fish when I finished up my violin practice. After Grandma tucked David in bed, read him a story, twice, and made sure the light was on in the hall, she poked her head into my room. "May I come in?"

"Uh-huh," I said.

"So, good night my little Itzhak Perlman."

"I'm not little." I winced. "And I'm not half as good as Perlman. I'm me."

"Someday, God only knows, there could be a proud grandmother somewhere saying to her grandchild, 'Good night, my little Jason Glass.' "

"Oh, Grandma." I groaned and rolled over, facing the wall.

"You never know," she said. "Stranger things could happen."

"Good night, Grandma," I mumbled from under the covers.

"Good night, *shana cup*." She kissed the bumpy lump where my head was underneath the blanket.

I tried to stay up until my mother came home from the P.T.A. meeting. As I waited, I thought of the week: Barney didn't care that Mr. Carr was gone. He called him a "homo." Tommy was no slouch, either. He said he was a "queer." My parents tell me that people are who they are *underneath*. What matters is if they are good and kind, and not mean and hurtful to others. As I lay here thinking, there was a part of me that didn't like admitting what I was feeling, because I liked Mr. Carr so much, but it seemed strange to me to like someone who was the same sex. I don't mean like as in how I like Caleb, I mean like in a sexual way. I don't really care if someone else does, I just know that it's something I don't feel.

It felt as though I had been waiting for hours when I finally heard the electric garage door go up, then down, and Mom's car door slam below my bedroom floor.

"Ma," I whispered as she peeked in on David.

She tiptoed into my bedroom, turning off the hall light. "Jason?"

"I'm up." Mom made her way in the semi-darkness toward my bed. I could smell the faint odor of her perfume. The moonlight lit the quilt she had sewn by hand after I was "toilet-trained and old enough for a bed."

"You're still up." She leaned over and kissed me on the forehead.

"How was the meeting?"

My mother let out a deep sigh. "It was awful."

"What happened?" I turned closer.

"Mrs. Rosenthal started in on Mr. Carr immediately. She said, 'He's leaving early. We should discontinue his health insurance and suspend his pension.' "

"What's that?"

"Some of his salary for retirement. Now, of all times! Caleb's mother argued, 'What about his loyalty to the school after all these years?' Parents started shouting at each other. Then the teachers got in the act. Some of them felt betrayed."

"Not Mrs. Jackson?" I asked.

"Of course not," Mom assured me. "She came to his defense. She stood up and said, 'Do you know what it's like being an African-American teacher in a mostly white school? I feel different every day. The point is, would we even be discussing this if he had any other illness?' She stared right at Mrs. Rosenthal and Tommy's father, who sat with his arms crossed over his chest."

"Did he say anything?"

"That Mr. Carr was morally unfit to be with children."

"Boy, is that mean! I can't believe he said that!"

Mom lowered her eyes, "Actually, he said, 'That fag shouldn't be near our kids.' The crowd got rowdy, and when things calmed down, the school board fielded questions. One of the fathers said he feared that Mr. Carr could have infected some of the students. So the school nurse and a pediatrician educated the audience on AIDS, how that was impossible."

"Is it?" I asked.

My mother nodded, adding, "I said that I hope they educate our children as well. I'd rather have my son knowledgeable and alive instead of ignorant and dead someday."

My mother bent down and gave me a butterfly kiss on my cheek. We both giggled. She tucked the blanket around my body, tight and close. "I always want to have you around," she said quietly. And she hugged me. When she did, what ran through my head was how Tommy must really miss his mother, and it must make him very angry at the world. I understood, but I still didn't like the way he was.

As her arms remained wrapped around me, she wiggled her toes against mine, just like when I was little. "Mr. Carr's going to die, isn't he?" I asked.

"He's had a life." She let out a deep breath. "Not as long as he imagined he would have, but he's lived more than some people who live until they're ninety. He's seen a lot."

"I've barely seen anything," I said.

"It's where we go in our head. I wouldn't say that you haven't seen anything. Your music takes you places that most people will never go to in their whole lives. It will sustain you forever through all sorts of times in your life. As a mother, I hope only for the good times."

"Me, too," I whispered.

"But I know that's impossible." Mom sighed.

"Would you walk me to the bathroom?" I asked.

"Sure," she said. We walked down the hall. Mom peeked in on David. She lifted his exposed foot and placed it under the blanket. "I love you guys."

"How much?" I teased.

My mother thrust her outstretched arms as wide as she could. I looked up at her. Her eyes were filled with tears. And when she walked me back into my room, she remained until our breathing formed a synchronized rhythm.

Friday morning Tommy said to Barney, loud enough for everybody to hear, "Mr. Carr's gone and he didn't even say good-bye."

When was the last time I had talked to Mr. Carr? At the chamber recital auditions? *I* never had a chance to say good-bye. I felt sad.

Wendy looked at me as I looked back at her. "Maybe he's got things on his mind," she said.

"Yeah, I bet he does," Tommy lashed out. "Like what *things*?"

"Things," I repeated. "What's the difference? It's *his* business."

"His business has become everyone's business," Tommy muttered.

"It didn't have to be. He has a right to his privacy," I said.

"He gave that up when he got this disease."

"No, he didn't," I answered him.

Mrs. Jackson raised her voice and said firmly, "This morning we have a special program about maturation. It happens to us all. Even the plants you've been growing. The girls will be spending time with Mrs. Richter, the school nurse. The boys with Coach Johnson." There were scattered giggles.

"Me and an avocado pit have a lot in common," Tommy chimed in.

"They do," someone in the back shouted out. The class laughed.

"Ask any questions you want answered. Take this opportunity. You can always ask me," she continued. Then she glared at Tommy. "Within reason."

The boys lined up and went to the gym. Coach was near the bleachers, next to a chart of The Male Reproductive System. He handed each boy a pamphlet called *Growing Up* as we filed by. He patted a few of us on the back as if we were here for a pep rally for a soccer match.

"Hi, guys," he said as the final rows in the back settled down. "I guess you'll have a lot to ask," he added as we thumbed through our booklets with diagrams of all private parts. There was dead silence, except for the sound of pages turning. "Can anyone in the room tell me some of the signs of puberty, that someone's body is maturing?"

"My brother has peach fuzz above his lips. My dad wants to know where his shaving cream is going to," Tommy shouted out.

"Good. Hair will also grow under your arms and on your legs."

"The werewolf syndrome." Tommy made loud sucking noises.

"Your voice will change," Coach added as Tommy growled like a wolf. "Become deeper, as Tommy is demonstrating for us." He smiled good-naturedly.

The entire room howled with laughter.

"I'm growing taller," Barney said. He was still pretty short.

"A growth spurt," Coach interjected.

Tommy waved his arm. "My brother also spends a lot of time in the bathroom with *Playboy* magazines."

"Does anyone know what hormone triggers puberty?" Coach asked.

Caleb raised his hand shyly. "Testosterone. I read about it in my mother's biology textbook."

"Excellent." Coach grinned at Caleb.

"I've heard of that." Tommy chuckled. "My father told my brother the other night that he had a bad case of testosterone when he yelled at Pop for no reason. He's acting so nuts, I think he's one big pus ball that should be zapped from the face of the earth with a giant Clearasil tube."

"Which brings up another indication of the

onset of puberty. The sebaceous glands." Coach wrote "sebum" on the blackboard. "An oily substance that clogs the pores of your skin and can combine with germs to form pimples," he said.

"Zits," Tommy spouted out. "What's that bump on your neck?" he said to Barney, who covered it self-consciously, probably thinking he had a humongous red pimple. "Your head!" Tommy slapped his knee and laughed.

Coach continued. "Testosterone will cause changes in your body. Pubic hair will grow. Your scrotum, testicles, and penis will all develop until eventually you will have your first nocturnal emission."

"Sounds like car talk," Tommy said to Barney.

"Semen, which is a mixture of sperm and other fluids, ejaculates during an involuntary erection." He grew a squiggle with a tail on the board. "The penis gets hard. There's nothing to worry about. It's normal and happens to all us guys. Now glance through the booklet, which is yours to keep. It goes into further detail. And then ask questions," Coach said.

Barney raised his arm slowly. "Coach Johnson? How come there's nothing in this booklet about AIDS? After last night's PTA meeting, shouldn't we know about that?"

I sank lower in my seat and felt all hot. The tips of my ears seemed as though they were on fire. Caleb nervously bounced his leg.

"Well"—Coach cleared his throat—"this booklet is mainly about the birds and the bees."

"Yeah, and that's about the bees and the bees." Tommy snickered.

"I was saying," Coach went on as he wiped the whiskers of his light gray mustache, "I agree with you, Barney. You should know the facts." He turned toward the blackboard and wrote:

How You Can Get AIDS.
1. Blood transfusion with HIV-infected blood
2. Drug user using unsterilized needle infected with the virus
3. Sexual contact with an infected partner
4. Babies born to infected mothers

"Any questions?" Coach looked at Barney.

"My mother said Mr. Carr has it. Does he?"

"Yes, he does," Coach answered.

Then questions started pouring out:

"Could you get it from using the water fountain?"

"If someone sneezed on me? Or coughed?"

"What about in the bathroom? Or lunchroom in the food?"

"What if I petted Mr. Hobbs, Mr. Carr's guinea pig?"

"How about a mosquito bite?"

"Yeah," Tommy said, "if an insect bites a homo, does that make him a fruit fly?" There were a few laughs around the room.

Coach paced and then moved closer to the

bleachers. "The answer to all your *questions*," and he emphasized the word "questions," glaring at Tommy, "is no. AIDS, which is different from other viruses, cannot be transmitted through casual contact. Only through an exchange of body fluids. Like blood, breast milk, semen, vaginal secretions."

"So I can get my ear pierced without worrying?" Wendell asked.

"By a doctor," Coach said, "using a sterilized needle. Okay?"

The bell rang and we all got up to leave. "Sit down," Coach said. "I recall Mr. Carr treated everyone in this gym to ice cream after the Jump-a-thon for the Heart Association last June. Some of you even had seconds. And thirds." Barney stared down at his sneakers. "Give the guy a break. He's your principal. He's been dedicated to each and every one of you. Remember that." Each of us clutched our pamphlet as we quietly filed out of the gym and back to the classroom. The girls and the boys could barely look at each other, and when we did, our eyes looked away.

During afternoon recess, while some people handed in their science projects and others fooled around on the computer, I went up to Mrs. Jackson. "Do you think," I hesitated, "you could help me get letters to Mr. Carr? I'd like to send him a poem or tell him what's going on."

"You could be our class reporter," she said, and smiled.

"Well"—I looked down at the speckled linoleum floor—"I was thinking of doing this on my own, and keeping the idea between us. Otherwise, everyone will keep bothering me about what to say, did he answer, and what he said. I want to write what I feel, like you told us to for the book we're going to make."

"I'll make sure he gets your letters or poems down South where he's staying now. You can seal them in an envelope if you want, and then give them to me to send. It's our secret," she whispered as I returned to my seat.

At the end of the day, Mrs. Jackson wished everyone a Merry Christmas and a Happy Chanukah as we dipped our hands one by one into a large grab bag filled with small gifts that each of us had wrapped.

"What did you get?" Caleb asked.

"A book on bugs," I said.

Caleb seemed disappointed. "I got a journal."

"Do you want to swap?" I asked.

His face lit up. "Thanks!" he shouted as my bus drove away. "I'll call you!"

I waved, watching his dark-green hooded parka flap in the wind.

When I got home, my mother was there and not at the restaurant.

"How come you're home?" I glanced at the recipe on the counter.

"I know, it's our busiest time of year catering

parties"—she drew in a deep breath—"but David's under the weather, and Grandma Fanny couldn't baby-sit. I'm making a special-order dessert right now. Here."

"I thought you hated making desserts." I tossed my backpack.

"Your father begged me. What I do for love." She dramatically batted her eyelashes. "And, for the record, it's doughy cookies I disdain. They stick to everything in sight." I looked at the recipe's title.

"Mole Ice Milk? What are the ingredients?"

"Moles, of course," she said with a straight face.

"Chilies and chocolate," I said, reading the list as I saw the grains of cocoa in the measuring spoon. "Like I had on my enchiladas."

Mom added a pinch of cinnamon into the ice-cream machine. "I'd check for mole fur if I were you. It's awful when it gets stuck between your teeth. I once had to floss for days."

"Eech!" I pretended to puke in the kitchen sink. "Ma-a-a!"

My mother dabbed some brown sugar on my tongue with her finger. "To get sweet thoughts." She chuckled. "How was school today?"

"We did a holiday grab bag. I got a journal."

"Nice," she said as I opened the freezer for her when she was done blending the ice cream. I helped her clean up the countertop, and then I stopped to hug her. She gave me the "what was that for?" look.

"I'm glad you're my mother," I said, looking up at her.

"I'm glad you're my son," she said, looking down. "Now tell me what else happened in school today."

"Oh, nothing." I shrugged.

"You're sure?" she prodded.

"Coach saw us in gym," I said just as the telephone rang.

Mom answered it, and from the way she smiled, I knew it was my father. "Sweetheart," she said, "I'm sorry, that was Dad. He's desperate for help at the restaurant. Could you stay with David? You're old enough. We'll continue this talk later. I want to know what Coach said. Okay?"

"No sweat," I said.

"Thanks," she mouthed, blowing me a kiss.

As soon as Mom left, David woke up from his nap and stumbled out of his room, dragging the last shreds of his old flannel baby blanket. His cheeks were bright red and his eyes looked like large glass marbles. He started to cry when he saw just me. I felt his head. It was hot. I got scared, but I didn't let David know.

"Would you like a bubble bath? Mom does that to cool me down."

He rubbed his eyes, nodded, went into his bedroom, and came out with an armful of plastic boats. He followed me into Mom and Dad's bedroom. I wrapped him in Dad's huge terry cloth bathrobe, and he waited on the toilet seat as I filled the tub with lukewarm water. When the bubbles began to grow, David begged to go in, so I lifted him into the tub and then held his small hand for balance until he sat down. "Yippee!" David yelled as a rubber shark hit a submarine I had made from a kit with my grandfather the year he died.

I rolled up the sleeves of my polo shirt, which were soaked by now, and dipped my hands into the soapy suds. "Attack!" I grumbled noises and crashed animals into the water. Soldiers splashed near David's stomach, which made him giggle. "You're a goofball," I teased.

"You're a doofball!" David shouted back over the running water.

"A what?" I squirted water near his chubby chest. A tiny brontosaurus hid in the fold of his thigh.

"A loofaball. A mothball." His head bobbed as he giggled, and I began laughing at him laughing. He looked like one of those toys people put in the rear window of their cars that go up and down while they drive. David put his fingers in the bubbles and dripped some soap on my head.

"This is war! Bombs away!" I cried, splashing him. I couldn't tell if he was going to laugh or cry, so I made a soapy horn on his head. "You look like a triceratops." I showed him his hair in Mom's makeup mirror. We both started to laugh and for that one moment I was really happy that David was my brother. I never wanted anything to happen to him. I decided to erase wish number six, that David would disappear.

Did Mr. Carr have a younger or older brother who felt that way? Or sister? I think that even when I hate David, and he is totally obnoxious, I'll remember how goofy he looked with these tomato cheeks and a soapy cone on his head.

After his bath, the fever caused David to nap again. While I listened for my mother's car, I took out the journal and wrote a poem.

MY CAY

Coconut trees line the sight of my cay,
With sap dripping down their trunks.
Palm fronds sway in the tree's grasp
Cooling the burning crystal sand.

Then I wrote a letter to Mr. Carr.

Dear Mr. Carr,
I hope you like the poem I'm sending you.
I wrote it after I read a book. Everyone wants
you to come back real soon. The substitute
principal, Ms. Mosely, is okay, but she
doesn't compare to you. She never tells jokes
over the PA, ever. And she doesn't let me keep
my violin under the desk like you did. She
said, "The school is not responsible for any
student's instrument. I can't make special
rules for one individual. It isn't fair to every-

one concerned. *What if the entire orchestra wanted to keep their violins or cellos under my desk or in my office?" Well, it's not* her *office, it's* yours. *"I'm the only one asking," I told her. "Rules are rules," she insisted. I remember you once said, "Rules are meant to be broken." I have to admit at the time, for a principal saying that, I thought you were kind of nutty, not to mention asking for trouble in a big way. Now that I know you better, I think you were saying we should learn to think for ourselves, be creative, and not be robots always following and doing exactly what we're told without questioning. Anyway, when I come back from vacation, I have to keep my violin in the orchestra room along with everyone else's. I'm looking forward to practicing the chamber ensemble when we go back to school in January. I don't think I'll be nervous the day of the performance because I noticed groups always use the music. It's not like when a soloist plays by heart alone on stage. That would be like performing in the circus without a net. Scary.*

Happy Near Year!

Jason Glass

After some violin practice, I fixed myself a big snack and then took a shower. As the water trickled down my stomach, I noticed six pubic hairs.

No, seven. Actually, one was a thread from the washcloth. Down to six again. Still, one more hair than last month. After I got into my sweatpants I heard my mother humming in her bedroom. I ran down the hall and plopped on the bed next to her. She turned away from the laundry she was folding and put the basket next to the night table. The book on AIDS was still there, next to some novels.

"So," my mother said while she flattened a rumpled T-shirt of David's, "what did Coach talk about in school today?"

"Stuff." I shrugged.

"What stuff? Gym stuff?" she said.

"Growing-up stuff. AIDS. I guess 'cause of the meeting."

"Meeting or no meeting, it's things you should know about. Feel comfortable with. Dad and I are here if you have any questions, and if you feel uptight asking us, which you shouldn't, there are people in school."

"I know." I smiled and she smoothed my hair with her hand.

"You and David are the most important people in the world to me. And Dad. Not much else counts, really."

"Not even getting the last piece of pizza, and extra cheese slid over from the slice next to it?" I joked.

"Well, after that, of course," she teased back.

We gave each other tickle torture until my

mother held her side and could barely breathe. "I give up," she gasped between breaths.

"Truce?" I asked, ready to give her one last tickle.

"Truce," she said.

I decided to tickle her anyway. I knew she'd still love me.

During the rest of the winter break, Caleb and I finished our science project one day, and played after a storm the next, building a fort until the sun set. Shadows reflected on the pale pink mounds surrounding us. It was as though we were swirling in peach sherbet. Caleb lay on the frozen surface, moving his arms and legs up and down, trying to make snow angels like the little gold ones dangling on the branches of his Christmas tree. I tiptoed across the drifts.

"I'm floating," I shouted, staying on the crusty surface.

"Me, too." His footsteps barely made a dent as he walked.

It was cold and dark by the time Caleb's mother picked him up in their van. Back inside, it felt good to take off my socks and sink my icy toes into the thick carpet. The air in the house was warm. Comforting. It was one of those times that I usually never think of, where I said to myself, I love my home. Being here. Protected. I felt lucky. And safe.

January

❧

Word was going around the playground that Mr. Carr would never be coming back. Kids in the lower grades seemed indifferent as they jumped rope and sang songs. They hadn't known Mr. Carr long enough to realize what they'd be missing over the years at Sherman Elementary. Some of the teacher aides had playground duty and chatted near the sandbox, gossiping about the winter break or what had happened to Mr. Carr. Life went on.

On Mondays, Mrs. Jackson always sounds hoarse when we sing "My Country 'Tis of Thee" because on Sundays she spends her time "belting out hymns" in the choir at the First Baptist Church on Main Street. Sometimes when we've stopped for bagels near the church before Hebrew school, I've seen her greeting the preacher outside.

"I hope everybody had a restful vacation." Mrs. Jackson cleared her throat and popped a cough drop in her mouth. "Those of you who've done the final touches on your science projects, please bring them to the long table in the back corner."

Caleb took over our oral report, fastened in a bright green binder, and placed it under our charts. He sighed with relief. I smiled.

"Finally," he said to me on his way back to his seat.

I hope we can work on another project together someday.

My parents had given the school permission for Miss Ryan to drive me up to the high school during lunch so that our chamber music group could meet for the first time.

"Hi." She grinned as I handed her the permission slip, which we turned in to the office before we left. I followed Miss Ryan to her car and slipped in the front seat after she moved a stack of textbooks, several tapes, and a paperback on taxidermy out of the way. I felt a little strange being with a teacher in a car. Well, she was almost a teacher, but still a student, so it was not as weird as it would have been with Mrs. Jackson.

When she turned the ignition on, rock music blasted. She looked embarrassed. "I won't tell anyone," I said. We both laughed.

She tapped the steering wheel. "How was your holiday?"

"I hung out," I said. "My parents are pretty busy that time of year with catering all those fancy Christmas and New Year's Eve parties."

"I sort of hung out, too. I skied Upstate for a day. Went to a comedy club. When is a door not a door?" She chuckled. "When it's ajar."

As she came up to a red light and paused, I asked, "Did you get a letter about Mr. Carr?"

She nodded.

"Do you think Ms. Mosely will be our permanent principal?"

"Your guess is as good as mine," she replied as we rounded the corner near the front entrance of the high school.

"You would have liked teaching under Mr. Carr. You are both—"

"Offbeat," she finished my sentence. "I've heard. Honestly, he sounds like a great guy. I'm sorry I didn't get to know him better."

I grasped the car handle. "Thanks for taking me," I said.

After I closed the door, she leaned over and rolled down the window. "Have a good one!"

"I don't think we're rehearsing yet. Mr. Andrews is just placing us in groups and probably giving out the music."

"Whatever. Have fun. See you later."

When I entered the music room, Mr. Andrews exclaimed, "Hold on."

He handed me a piece by Vivaldi, and I sat down.

"You look disappointed," said the boy next

to me. I recognized him from the audition.

"I played this one at my music camp over a summer."

"So tell him."

"It's okay," I shrugged. "I should be happy just to be here."

"Different people will be working together. It won't sound the same," he said. "A year or two makes a big difference. You'll see."

"You're right. And there's a Haydn quartet, too. I like Haydn."

"I have one also. Let's see if it's the same score. It is!" He put out his hand to shake mine. "My name is Shihung Li. Remember Mr. Carr did tai chi at Sherman when I first came to this country?"

"Yes." I nodded. "The violist. I remember."

"I don't see him here today. This chamber thing is his baby."

"He's no longer at Sherman."

"He's not? Tough luck."

"Yeah," I said, letting out a deep sigh.

"Where did he go? To another school?"

"To Virginia," I said.

"It's warm."

"Yeah, it's warm," I repeated, looking sadly down at the music.

I hoped I would feel excited enough about playing without Mr. Carr around.

"What's the difference between a viola and a violin?" he asked. Without missing a beat, he answered, "A viola takes longer to burn."

"Another dumb viola joke?" I asked.

He nodded. "How do you know when a concert stage is level?"

"How?" I asked, going along with him.

"When the violist is drooling out of both sides of his mouth."

I didn't laugh. I felt like David, who didn't get my jokes.

"Come on, most musicians think it's a big violin for people who couldn't make it at the violin."

"A violin for klutzes," I said.

"For what?" he asked.

"Clumsy people. Though I don't think that's true about violists. I like the sound of the viola. It is deep and rich."

"My parents don't want me to be a musician anyway they want me to be a doctor."

"My parents want me to be whatever I want to be."

He looked at me strangely.

We quickly formed groups before the bell rang.

"Practice your parts. We'll meet again as soon as I can get you all together in one spot," Mr. Andrews said matter-of-factly.

Miss Ryan was waiting for me in her old red car out front.

"Everything go okay?" she asked. "You don't look very inspired."

91

"Mr. Andrews isn't Mr. Carr. I've been waiting to do these chamber groups with Mr. Carr since I began the violin in third grade."

"Well . . ." Miss Ryan sighed. "Maybe when you rehearse, and later perform, you could play as though Mr. Carr were there?"

Miss Ryan got me thinking. "Or maybe I should play for me without worrying about anyone or anything because it's something *I* need to do. Then I think I'd really be doing what Mr. Carr wanted all along."

"Jason," she said with a smile, "that's a much better thought than mine."

I felt grateful to her as she drove me back to school. I got back just in time for Mrs. Jackson to give out the homework assignment.

That night, after thinking about the day, and what Miss Ryan had said, I wrote another letter.

Dear Mr. Carr,

Sorry you're still not back. I told you that Ms. Mosely doesn't tell jokes, sing songs, or read poetry over the PA system in the morning. She recites the pledge of allegiance to the flag with us, then abruptly gives the day's messages and gets off. She patrols the cafeteria at lunchtime and doesn't let people from one class sit with people from another. Is that crazy or what? Caleb Harmon says, "She's all business." By the way, we did a science project on photosyn-

thesis. I was wondering if you would like me to check on your rubber tree. It must be enormous by now. You should have taken it with you to a southern climate, but then maybe you'll be back to enjoy it? We formed chamber groups today.

Best wishes to you,

Jason Glass

P.S. Mr. Hobbs has been adopted by the kindergarten. I think they are overfeeding him, or else maybe he's a Mrs. Hobbs. Miss Ryan, our student teacher, thinks so. One of the girls brought him to her house over the winter vacation. She already had another guinea pig, and kept them in a cage together. It seems a Hobbs family might be in the works. Baby guinea pigs would be so exciting!

The next two weeks our class was busy every day with a different person or group giving their science report. The day Caleb and I gave ours, we each got an A. We celebrated at the Scoop Shoppe afterward.

"The usual," I said to Henry, the manager.

"One brownie special with raspberry sherbet and hot fudge?"

I nodded as Caleb said, "A scoop of vanilla."

"Nothing on it?" Henry asked, making sure.

"Just plain." He smiled, looking satisfied as

Henry handed him his scoop. I would have needed at least sprinkles.

Each afternoon, I picked up the mail after I got off the school bus, wondering if today would be the day I received a letter from Mr. Carr. I hoped Mrs. Jackson had mailed mine to him. And if she did, why couldn't he have answered me? Should I try writing again, or was I bothering him?

After we rehearsed, I wrote another letter. Even if I didn't get an answer, writing to him made me feel better.

> *Dear Mr. Carr,*
>
> *I thought I'd let you know how the chamber group is going. Alexandra Wheaton is the first violinist. I am the second violinist. I'm excited to play with her. Maybe she will tell me what it was like at the Aspen Music Festival. She's so good, I'm trying to keep up with her. She plays with a lot of strength. When I try to get as much sound as she gets, my arm hurts. I have to build up those muscles. My teacher says I will as I use more vibrato and martelé. I tell myself that I have a lot of years to sound as good as Alexandra, but I sort of want it now. Is that wrong?*
>
> *We were supposed to be a quartet, but now we have a pianist accompanying us. Her name is Reiko Nakame. She's an exchange student from Japan, a seventh-grader. She*

moved here recently because her father was transferred by the bank he works for. She speaks little English, but learned enough in school to tell us that she practices until eleven. Mr. Andrews called her playing "technically flawless." She always knows exactly when to come in. I dropped my music on the floor today during rehearsal and Mr. Andrews gave me a look when I fumbled to pick up the sheets near my stand. We had to begin again. I felt really bad.

Minsoo Kim is the cellist. Why do tall, lanky people pick the cello? I don't think I've ever seen a chunky cellist. I like to watch her as she plays. She has a lot of feeling and expression in her face. She moves her body with the instrument, as though they were doing a dance. Her ponytail swings. Sometimes her glasses slide down her nose from beads of sweat. I have to keep from laughing because she's using both her hands to play and can't possibly push them back up, so they remain perched on the tip of her nose. They never seem to fall off.

Shihung, who you already know, is the violist, but is really going to be a doctor someday. At least his parents think so. I like him a lot. He always cracks jokes in the group and lets us lighten up.

All in all, I feel honored that you and Mr. Andrews asked me to be a part of this group. When I stop and think, I realize that

I'm still in the sixth grade and here with them. What will I be playing at their age? Where? I never think, will I be playing? I know I will. Always.

Time to go to sleep,

Jason Glass

P.S. Why shouldn't you iron a four-leaf clover? Because you shouldn't press your luck. (Caleb told me that one. It's going around the classroom now.)

The last week in January, Mr. Carr sent a video to the school. The upper grades gathered for an assembly. He was in a hospital, wearing striped pajamas, and looking surprisingly cheerful. I still hadn't heard from him.

"At least he's not wearing one of those gowns that are open in the back with his butt exposed," Tommy cried out when the lights went low and the tape began.

I thought of Pajama Day a few months ago, and of two summers ago when he was swimming in the lap lane next to me at the town pool. At the time, I couldn't believe I was seeing my own principal in a bathing suit. And now, once again, in pajamas. But this occasion wasn't a celebration like Pajama Day had been. And Mr. Carr looked very different now.

"Hello, everyone at Sherman." Mr. Carr smiled and carefully took a sip through a straw in a cup that a nurse handed to him. "This is my pal, Nurse Battle-ax," he teased.

She patted him lightly on the arm and grimaced in a playful way. "And this is my worst patient. He organized a strike. Wanted spicy Italian meatballs and sauce force-fed through the IV tube."

Grandma Fanny probably would have wanted to do that with matzoh balls for Grandpa when he was sick and didn't feel like eating.

There were a few brown spots on Mr. Carr's face. His hair had thinned a little in patches. Otherwise, it was Mr. Carr. Twinkling eyes and a big smile. The camera panned the room: Flower baskets. Handmade get-well cards Scotch-taped all over the wall. Letters piled high. Maybe one of them was mine? I hope he'd answer soon.

February to March

❦

My mother called February to the end of March "the mud and bud season." I stepped over melting snow onto the muddy lawn. My boots sank. Caleb was trying to patch the remains of our fort and the few half-frozen blocks left from February storms. The fort had been almost as tall as Caleb and me. We crawled through a tunnel on our bellies like worms until our snowsuits were soaked with brown ice and mush. When we weren't playing outside, we were inside, either at home or in school, and always busy. Most of the time, it felt like inside, even during recess. Ms. Mosely called it "Indoor Noontime." I was waiting for spring. I was also waiting to hear from Mr. Carr. Was he wrapped up with himself right now, and just trying to get through each day? I stopped writing because I didn't want to make a pest of myself. I missed him at the chamber practices. They were going pretty well. He would have been happy, I think.

Maybe even a bit surprised. The solo was going to be one or two movements from the Bach Concerto no. 2 in E Major. My father was going to buy me the music so I could practice for the audition.

Wendy began organizing the final book of our art and poems for Mr. Carr with help from Miss Ryan. Mrs. Jackson said, "This will be something he can save." *Save*—that sounded good to me. Mrs. Jackson brought in handmade paper pressed from African tree bark. We attached the paper to the binding board with thick white paste. This was the poem I decided to include:

LIVING BEINGS

Living beings roam from rocky shores,
To where they dwell for food and shelter.
From huge to small, lions to mice,
They forge through fields, not caring hot or cold.
During winter's passage, some dare not go out,
But to others, it's a time of play.
Though humans destroy and construct,
They also regard wisdom and life,
Of every creature around them.

Before Wendy and Miss Ryan were almost done, it was time to go to "specials." Some of the class went to TESL, Teaching English as a Second Language, others to remedial reading or speech, while one group went to band and another to orchestra. I grabbed my gray canvas violin case from among the standard black leather-looking plastic ones in the bottom of the coat closet and headed for the music room in the basement. Mr. Andrews came down from the high school to teach music on Wednesdays. He was tuning the string instruments to the piano while I tuned my own by ear. "Jason, could you help me with a few?" he asked.

I walked over to Barney, who struggled to turn the peg of his G string. "If you put a little soap on the wood inside the peg, it might move a little easier." Barney glared at me. "I'm serious. But not too much, or else your string will keep slipping and go out of tune."

"Sure, Jason. I'll give my violin a bubble bath."

"Have it your way." I shrugged.

"Actually, everyone in your family likes it *your* way."

"What does that mean?" I narrowed my eyes.

"Oh, nothing."

I felt my palm sweating around the neck of my violin as I held it firmly by my side. "You said something, back it up."

"My mother said that your mother made such a stink about Mr. Carr's rights. Who cares? What about *our* rights? Endangering our health."

"He hurt no one's health. You heard Coach. And so did I."

"Tommy said he's a fag," Barney shot back.

"You're a jerk, Barney. Why don't you think

before you say stupid things? There must be a synapse missing between your brain and lips." Then I muttered under my breath, "Did I ever tell you you're a fat little turd?" Barney's eyes widened. His short black hair glistened with sweat. He nearly whacked his already nicked violin against the metal orchestra chairs as he hastily moved away. Was he going to tell on me? My heart was pounding. So was my head. What if Mr. Andrews kicked me out of the chamber recital? I felt meaner than Barney because of all the nasty thoughts that were circling through my mind for him and people like him. Narrow, stupid, pea-brained people.

I practiced the music for the spring concert without listening to the sound, just going through the motions. My heart and my head were elsewhere. A tiny hidden place that wished for life when I knew there would be none. The same spot it had been for Grandpa. I was also scared for me.

The bell rang. We packed up our instruments and left them in the crowded orchestra room. I carefully placed mine slightly away from the others, so it wouldn't get run over when everyone rushed out at once to be first on the lunch line. Barney waddled down the hall. I couldn't even look as I passed him and sat down next to Caleb in the cafeteria.

"How was band?" I asked.

Caleb beat a rhythm on his brown paper bag. "The saxophones are getting a few bars highlighted in the piece we're playing for the spring concert. Josh, Pam, and I get to stand up alone for a couple of measures."

"Great," I said.

"You don't sound like it's great."

"It is. It's just that Barney pissed me off at rehearsal. He started in about Mr. Carr."

"Barney and his mother act like they've gotten the raw end of the deal, so they want everyone else to have nothing, too."

Caleb went back to playing the table like a drum with his two forefingers as I silently chewed my sandwich. When I finished, I took a sip of my drink and said, "You play a mean table." I answered him with a beat of my own against the long bench.

"You play a mean bench." He crumpled some waxed paper in his bag.

We headed outside. Tommy and Barney were hanging out with a bunch of friends near the lunchroom exit. I felt hard inside as we edged through the corridor next to them. As soon as Caleb and I walked by, they stopped talking. Their silence felt loud. I wanted to say that I hated the way they were. Instead, I held in my frustration and decided I would add to my list of wishes: 11) *I wish Barney would never again come in the car pool for Hebrew school*, and 12) *I wish Tommy would get a tooth abscess*, so he'd shut his mouth.

When we were finally outside, I heard them

whistle at us and then giggle. It was incredibly dumb, but I still felt hot with embarrassment.

"Hi, guys," Tommy sang. "Always see you two together."

"You, too," Caleb said in a singsong voice to him and Barney.

Caleb and I walked around the school yard. We no longer watched for them. We shifted our attention to the anthills and buds beginning to break through cracked earth. Crocuses had burst in a rock garden outside the main office. Mr. Carr's desk had faced the window overlooking it, probably so he could see the flower bed with its changing seasons. Ms. Mosely had moved the desk away from the window.

Mr. Carr had the entire school plant a tulip bed when a first-grader got hit by a car and was killed. Every spring he made sure we raked away the dead leaves left over from the winter so that it looked nice, and we could see the bronze plaque in the ground with Patrick Shutler's name on it. Today as Caleb crouched over a pile of dry leaves, moving them with a short twig to clear the plaque, I said, "I'll be right back."

I made my way up the steps to the boys' bathroom. On the way, I passed the music room. The door was wide open. That was odd. Mr. Andrews always kept it closed. I searched for my violin in the sea of others and didn't see it. There was a sudden sharp pain in my chest, as if my heart had stopped.

Then thumping. My legs began to tremble from fear as I walked through the maze of black cases. I was in a cold sweat. Then I smiled with relief as I saw it off in the back, under a large desk. False alarm. My shivering stopped. It must have been pushed aside as we all left for lunch, I thought. A corner of my white handkerchief was draped outside the zipper, which seemed strange to me. I didn't think I had left it like that. I had to go to the bathroom, but somehow, that didn't seem as urgent now as checking my violin. I tried to tug open the zipper and get the cloth out from between the teeth, but I couldn't without ripping my grandpa's handkerchief. I sighed, knowing I still had a few left at home, but now, I had one less thing of his. When I opened the case, I fell to my knees onto the cold linoleum floor. My violin was smashed. The neck was broken. All the strings were cut. The bridge had been destroyed with something blunt. Chalk was grated along the fingerboard. Razorlike grooves were etched along the swirls of the wood grain. The soundpost had been attacked with a hammer or a pocketknife. Now I noticed in the distance the pegs tossed about the floor. Why hadn't I seen them before? I carefully picked them up and sat there, numb, immobilized, holding them in my hands, grasping them tightly until my nails dug into my skin. The tiny door to the compartment that held my small box of rosin was ripped off. White Elmer's Glue had been dripped inside, all over the round purple cake.

Suddenly, I scooped up everything and ran upstairs to my classroom, where I knew I would be alone. I went to the back of the coat closet and sat on the floor beneath the hook that held my backpack and jacket. My mother had forced me to wear a woolen hat, too, and I had been annoyed. She had said, "Wear it, it's nippy." I wanted her now, this very second, close to me. I wanted my father, too. But I was alone. I rocked back and forth.

Strings of clear mucus dripped from my nose as I cried, making wet puddles on my jeans. Who would do such an awful thing? Tommy? Barney? Hadn't Barney learned anything from the rabbi in Hebrew school about good and evil? I couldn't believe, even with all the things Tommy and Barney had said, or I had said to Barney during orchestra, that either of them would do something so mean. Could I be wrong? And not know them at all? What really went on inside? Wasn't that how Barney's mother had treated Mr. Carr? Were we all like clocks, with clean precise faces we show to the world and intricate workings inside? Never truly knowing each other?

I looked up and stared into Miss Ryan's concerned face.

"Jason," I heard her say off in the distance, "what happened?"

I held my hands open. The pegs rolled onto the floor. The strings curled on my lap. She stared at the fragments in my case and wiped my cheeks

105

with a tissue, which she had quickly taken from her purse.

"I came from the teachers' room," she said. I stared at her blankly. "The faculty lunchroom next door," she continued, "and I was talking about the poetry we're writing for Mr. Carr. The other teachers wanted to see the book we're making before we mail it out."

I picked up the pegs like pieces from a jigsaw puzzle, hoping they would fit to make the picture whole.

"Speak to me, Jason." Miss Ryan put her arms around me.

I couldn't find the words.

Miss Ryan led me down to Ms. Mosely's office. I waited outside the closed door with the school secretaries as I overheard them paging Mrs. Jackson to the principal's office. Miss Ryan finally opened the door and motioned for me to come in when Mrs. Jackson arrived. "Are you okay?" Mrs. Jackson asked with concern as soon as she saw me. I nodded and went behind the high, long counter that separated the world of students and teachers, and entered Ms. Mosely's office. Mr. Hobb's hutch was gone from the corner. So was the bust of Mozart and the ceramic statue of Mickey Mouse. They had been replaced by a snake plant, the pot still wrapped in gold foil.

"Do you know who did this?" Ms. Mosely almost shouted.

I shook my head no.

Miss Ryan looked quickly at Mrs. Jackson, then down at the floor, pausing, and then back up at Ms. Mosely. Ms. Mosely waited, examining me like a specimen under a microscope. I didn't want to be sitting here answering questions. Let her find who did this and answer whatever she wanted to know. She hadn't let me keep my violin in a safe place.

"I'd like to call my parents," I said, clutching my case.

I don't want to be here, I thought. Ever again. I want to go home.

Ms. Mosely poked her head outside and said to her secretary, "Find Jason Glass's emergency contact card and notify his parents to come to school as soon as possible. Also let them know that he's safe."

Mrs. Jackson smiled gently. "I've got to go back to the classroom. I'll send a monitor with your things. Don't worry about homework tonight. You're excused. Do you want Miss Ryan to stay with you?"

"I'm here." Miss Ryan patted my knee. "The book can be put together anytime before graduation."

I wanted it done now. Every day counted. I felt as though Mr. Carr's life was like the glass timer I used when I played Perquacky with my parents. When I turned the timer upside down, the grains of salt spilled quickly as I spelled as many words as I could within a minute, until all the salt settled at the bottom, some grains clinging to the sides. My turn was over when the top was empty.

"It's okay," I said, letting Miss Ryan know she could go.

"I know it's okay." She waited on the bench next to me.

Both my parents came. I felt awful. Who was taking care of things at the restaurant? But I was also glad that they were both here. My father bent down and hugged me. His apron was still on, stained with some sauce. My mother knelt at my side. Her cheeks were flushed.

"Are you okay?" she gasped, looking confused.

Dad's eyes darted quickly from me to Miss Ryan. "What happened?"

I opened my case and showed them the fragments of my violin.

Mom began to tremble. "I thought something had happened to *you*."

"It did," I raised my voice.

"Yes, Sweetheart, it did, but thank God *you're* okay."

"I'm not okay." I shook with rage.

"*You're* in one piece." My father squeezed my shoulder.

My mother pressed her wet cheek against mine. Our tears fused. She whispered in my ear, "*You* can't be replaced."

My parents gave me a sandwich hug with me in the middle, and that's when I started to sob, hidden between them.

"Do you want to go home?" Ms. Mosely came out and asked. It was the first time I had seen her smile.

"Yes," I said softly.

"I'll sign you out." She turned to my parents, "We'll try to get to the bottom of this."

Miss Ryan introduced herself. "Hi, I'm Jason's assistant teacher. He's a lovely boy."

"Thank you," my parents both said.

I tried to smile at her as my father picked up the handle of my torn case, holding it tightly. "It'll be okay." He glanced down at me.

I looked up as we left the school. "How can I be in the Chamber Music Recital? Or practice? What about the spring concert in May?"

"We'll rent one until we can afford to buy another one."

"But, Dad, they sound awful." I felt defeated. "How can I try out for the solo without mine?"

My mother's shoulders went up and down as she began to cry. I put my arm around her waist. The suede from her belt felt warm. I rubbed my fingers across the smooth, fuzzy surface. It felt like the small "Play on Air" pillow that I sometimes rest between my shoulder and the violin when I play. I ached with sadness and felt empty about losing what was like a friend.

When I got home, I crawled under the cool, soft quilt on my bed. My body warmed it as I drifted off to sleep. Moonlight was shining through my half-drawn shades when I woke up and heard the distant murmur of my parents' voices. My throat was dry. And then I remembered. My violin. The image of the pieces, scattered.

Weeks after Grandpa died, I'd wake up in the morning, open my eyes, and feel okay. Then it would suddenly hit me. What had happened. And I'd no longer feel the same. I felt unsteady. Almost dizzy. Not complete. It took me awhile to belong to the world again and do ordinary things, simple acts, like go to the supermarket with my mother, or even play with a friend. Tonight felt similar.

I curled up into a ball and tucked the covers under my toes, never wanting to leave the safety of my bedroom: the hooked rug; the rocking chair Mom had found at a thrift shop, worn in the seat where I often sat reading or doing my theory home-work; Grandpa's olive-colored footlocker, from when he was in the army during World War II, which Mom had painted white and made into a toy chest at the end of my bed; a stick-figure drawing I did the night David was born of how our family looked with four people in it. I painted David purple. He looked like a monster baby.

I began to write a letter in my head to Mr. Carr, telling him about today. Then I put it down on paper.

110

Dear Mr. Carr,

Today was one of the worst days of my life. I was stripped of something that is a part of me. That, in a way, is me. My violin is me. It is my voice. How I feel. How I think. I can't exactly explain the feelings because they are so deep, but if I had to put them into words, I'd say that I don't know where the music begins and where I end. We merge into one as my body feels and hears the sounds I make with a simple piece of wood and strings. Today that dream was smashed. A human being smashed my violin. I overheard my mother ask my father, "What kind of a person does something like this? What kind of people are there in this world, who are so angry and hurtful?" My father answered her, "Pity them." They both look for the good, because that's the way they are, and it's the only way to survive. Tonight, I can't find goodness in people. Maybe tomorrow.

Wish you were here,

Jason Glass

There was a light tap at my bedroom door. "Jason? Jason darling, are you okay?" Mom tiptoed in and sat on the edge of my bed.

I leaned over the letter to Mr. Carr, hiding it with my arm.

My mother flipped the bangs up off my fore-

head, bent down, and kissed me. "You feel warm."
She pressed her lips against my forehead.

"I've been under a blanket for a few hours."

My mother stroked my arm. "Feel a tiny bit
better?"

"Not really," I answered, feeling an ache in my
stomach.

"Do you know who did it?" my mother asked.
"I know you wouldn't say in front of the principal,
but do you have any suspicions?"

I paused, tossing the blanket off of my arms.

"You can tell me. It will remain between us.
And Dad, of course."

"I'm not sure. Maybe Tommy. Or Barney. Or
both. They're mad at me about Mr. Carr."

My mother looked puzzled. "How are you
responsible for Mr. Carr?"

"That I'm on his side. You know."

"Tell me about it." She sighed. "I know." Mom
hugged me. "Jason, there's a part of me that
doesn't care if they find out who did this or not, as
long as you are left alone."

"I care," I said. "They should pay for it."

"Life doesn't always work out where bad people are punished and good people are rewarded.
Look at Mr. Carr. Some people in town think he
got what he deserved. Others don't. I have to live
with my own conscience. And so do you. In the
end, whoever did this to your violin has to live
with theirs. They have to get up each morning and

look at themselves in the mirror. I think that we all make choices about the paths we decide to take. They don't always turn out exactly like we want them to, tied up in a neat package with a silk ribbon on top, but that doesn't mean we should give up. You'll get another violin. Maybe even a better one, someday. Even though I believe in choices, there's a corner of my heart that also believes in fate," my mother said, tugging the blanket.

I scratched nervously at the arm of my sweatshirt. My mother grabbed my hand to stop me. "What's the matter?"

"I need to practice," I said in a whiny tone.

"Tonight?" She seemed surprised.

"Not tonight, but soon. The concert is in about a month or so. Right after the spring vacation. Maybe I shouldn't bother with the solo?"

"I don't want to hear talk like that," she said. "We'll go tomorrow after school to rent one."

"I have Hebrew." I thought of Barney and the car pool, and how I wanted more than ever for my wish number eleven to come true. Would I be able to tell by just looking in his eyes if he was innocent or guilty?

"Well," she said, looking up at the shining stars on my ceiling, "first thing when you get up? The music store opens at nine-thirty."

I smiled. "Thanks, Ma."

"I think everyone will understand if you're a little late."

"I agree," I said. "And I don't care if they don't."

"Want any dinner?" Mom asked.

"I'm not hungry."

"I made your favorite. Lemon chicken stuffed with rice pilaf."

"A small piece," I said. Mom seemed happy now. I added, "You look like you won a big prize."

"I did, you." And she went into the kitchen to reheat dinner.

Before I followed her, I took out my wish list for Mrs. Jackson and put number thirteen, an unlucky number on the bottom:

13) *I wish today never happened. Period.*

Then I changed it to I wish I had my violin back.

Caleb saw me at gym handing a late pass to Coach. "I heard what those scuzzballs did," he said. "I thought you weren't coming to school today when you didn't show up this morning."

"My mother took me to rent a violin. It had steel strings on it! I'll have to change it to my extra set of nylon ones tonight."

Caleb shook his head. "Forget it right now and play some ball."

Coach gave me a position in the outfield. Caleb

was the third baseman. Barney was up at bat. Caleb prowled third, watching second, while Barney continued to strike out. After we changed sides and it was my turn, Tommy tossed the baseball from his hand to his catcher's mitt and yelled out behind me as he threw the ball back to the pitcher, "Hey, Glass, you're bowing arm won't help you now!" Barney laughed. I got so mad, I put all my anger into the bat and hit a home run.

Caleb couldn't contain himself. "Too bad you were busy running. It would have been worth it to walk the home run just to see their faces. Especially since it's the first time in a long time that we're on the winning team." This made the next moment even worse. The bell for a fire drill sounded. Coach quickly lined us up in single file to walk to the other side of the playground, where everyone from inside the school poured out of the exit doors. As I rushed with everyone else, I noticed Tommy's mitt left on the bench near the dugout. In the confusion of the game and the drill, he must have forgotten it. After Ms. Mosely announced for us all to return inside, I realized Tommy still didn't have his mitt. That was when I had the idea to check the bench before I headed for the bus at the end of the day. When I did, it was still there, the leather soaked from the drizzle of rain mixed with a tiny bit of sleet. I stuffed the mitt in my backpack.

When I got home, my mother was in the kitchen. "I'm making vegetable dumplings for some corporate cocktail party. I could use a little help." She looked at me pleadingly.

"Sure," I said. "First I want to put my stuff away." I gleefully stared at Tommy's treasured possession on my bed, water stained, the leather beginning to crack. I put it near the radiator to dry.

When I came back into the kitchen and began to scoop the dumpling mixture, I heard a car horn beep. "I forgot," Mom said, "Hebrew school. Go. And wear a raincoat!" she shouted after me.

Barney didn't look me in the eye when I got into the backseat. I didn't look at him, either. I decided to no longer pay attention to him. That's what I do with people who hurt me or let me down. I wipe them off the face of the earth. To protect myself. I wondered as I sat in the car, did he wreck my violin? Did Tommy? Was it important to know? Wasn't it important that I continue to play? That I went on. And succeeded. And yet, it still was very painful.

Is there a time in life or afterward when we all have to face what we've done? I thought of some of the things I had done: teasing and torturing David. Years ago, watering down my mother's expensive perfume when she wouldn't let me sleep over at Caleb's. Being angry at Grandpa because I couldn't have an eighth birthday party. He was very sick by then and Mom's mind was elsewhere. As he stayed over in my bedroom, I brought in a lopsided birthday cake that Mom and I had baked, chocolate with apricot filling, and he tried to help me blow out the candles as the wax dripped onto the icing, but he couldn't. He was too weak and tired. He died during Rosh Hashanah, the Jewish New Year, when everyone begins the year by starting again with a fresh clean slate.

The year before, after synagogue, Grandpa and I had walked to a narrow canal from his beach bungalow. Outdoor motorboats lined the wooden piers that jutted from small sloping backyards. We tossed bread crumbs beyond the tall reeds that edged the shore and watched them work their way toward the bay. I told Grandpa I was sorry for saying to my father that I wanted to get rid of my little brother. Dad had glared at me like I was the kid from the movie *The Omen*. But when he told Mom, she laughed because she knew I'd never do a thing like that. Grandpa and I had stayed near the water until sunset as the seagulls swooped after the bread crumbs, scooping up the imaginary sins that we cast away downstream toward the ocean beyond.

Now all I could think about was what I wanted to do to Tommy's mitt. I thought of running a blade across the leather. Ripping open the stitching. Chopping off the glove's fingers with a sushi knife, putting them in my parents' Cuisinart and returning them to Tommy in a Baggie, liquefied. The list went on. What would Grandpa think of me now? Or Dad?

April

I overheard Tommy say to Barney, "It's April Fools' Day, and some fool stole my mitt."

Caleb looked at me. When we were alone, I said in a low voice, "I took it."

"You what?" He raised his eyebrows.

"He left it during the fire drill. I borrowed his mitt, and I guess I forgot to return it."

"Are you going to keep it?" Caleb asked me.

"I don't know. I think I'm going to let him squirm for a while, wishing he could have it back, wondering what he's going to do at lunchtime."

"An eye for an eye?" Caleb said.

"No, a mitt for a violin. And a mitt's a whole lot cheaper."

"What if he didn't do it?"

"What if he did?" I said.

"What if Barney did? Or he put Barney, that wimp, up to it since he's in orchestra with you? Taking Tommy's mitt won't hurt Barney."

"Maybe not, but it feels good right now."

"How is taking Tommy's mitt going to make things change? Your violin is still gone."

"It's not gone. It didn't disappear. It was destroyed, Caleb."

Caleb remained silent. We ended the conversation right there because he could see I wasn't going to budge.

In class, Miss Ryan looked happy as she put the finishing touches on the poetry book for Mr. Carr. She'd had color Xerox copies made of our art. We kept the originals. Mrs. Jackson grinned from ear to ear when she saw it covered with the special paper she had bought. She included a note to Mr. Carr with the book: "An early edition hot off the press!" She said to us, "The rest of you should have yours done before graduation." I stared proudly at my poem next to the illustration I had drawn, because it looked different bound inside a book. I was excited to make my own copy to keep.

My mother picked me up after school and drove me straight to Mrs. Lee's for a lesson. The first one I'd be having on the rented violin.

"Let's see," Mrs. Lee said calmly, taking the violin from me. "Your mother called and told me what happened." She turned the violin over and plucked a few strings. "Hmm. Could be worse."

"Could be better," I said. "I'm not used to the sound or the feel of the strings. Especially how the bow sounds with this violin. The whole combination doesn't feel right. My bow was left alone. Probably no one saw it tucked in the top lid of the case." I sighed. "What should I do?"

"Your best," she said, handing me back the instrument.

"But it sounds too fuzzy to project the kind of sound I want for the solo audition. I don't think I can do my best."

Mrs. Lee looked at me. "There will be many recitals, with wonderful violins. Learn to feel comfortable in public. Let this be your aim right now. The rest will fall into place. Naturally, I want you to sound good at your tryout, but . . ." her voice drifted off, "under the circumstances, don't drive yourself crazy. Now, let's work."

A week before the spring break I got a note from Mr. Andrews announcing the solo audition date the following Friday. I was very nervous about practicing and seemed to make more mistakes than less. "Try your best." I heard Mrs. Lee's words in my head, but I knew she didn't like to settle for fumbled notes. Neither did I.

On the morning of the audition, I stayed home with an upset stomach. I clipped my fingernails short as my mother drove me straight to the high school and dropped me off before she headed to the restaurant. "Here's a late note to give to Mrs. Jackson when you get back to your classroom. You'll do fine." She touched the dark red mark I'd made on the side of my chin from practicing so much. I closed the car door and turned, making my way up the steps without looking back.

There was a feeling of electricity in the air as each of us waited for our turn. My heart started beating harder as the first person went in the room to play. Some listened with their ear pressed to the door. I paced in small circles, silently moving my fingers as I played the notes of the movement.

"Take it easy." Shihung rested his broad hands on my shoulders.

"Take it easy? I'm next," I said.

"Will getting uptight make you play better? I can almost hear the adrenaline pumping through your body," he joked.

"So what should I do, old pro?" I looked at him for advice.

"Focus. Tune everyone out, except you and the music. That's all you should care about right now." He smiled with calm assurance.

"Are you a violist or a football coach?"

Before he answered me, I heard my name. "Next, Jason Glass."

"*Hao yunn*," Shihung said, patting my back. "Good luck in Chinese."

My insides were pounding as the accompanist poised her fingers on the white keys and watched for a sign from me that I was ready to begin. I wiped my palm on the leg of my good suit pants, twice, held the violin under my chin, adjusted the handkerchief, and nodded to begin. When it ended, the back of my white shirt was soaked. I was relieved it was over.

"Thank you." Mr. Andrews smiled. And that was it until I left the room and heard him call, "Next, Shihung Li."

"*Mazel tov*," I whispered as he passed. "Good luck in Yiddish."

There was one expression I knew from Grandma without any help.

I changed into the jeans that I had put in my backpack before the school van drove me back to Sherman Elementary. No one realized I was late, because they were busy working. Maybe Caleb, but he only looked up and waved. The only person in that entire school who would have known the importance of what I had done was Mr. Carr.

And then of course my parents. The phone was ringing as I walked in the door. "How'd you do?" my mother asked, sounding out of breath.

"Okay," I said, hearing the clatter of pots and pans in the background.

"Okay?" she repeated.

"Fine, Ma. I'll find out who got it after the vacation."

"I'll be home soon. I got caught up in a vegetable soufflé," she said.

"Sounds messy. Hope you can get out," I teased her.

"Very funny," she said. "That sounds like my old Jason."

"And you sound like my old ma," I teased her again.

During every spring vacation, Caleb went to Massachusetts to celebrate Easter with his grandparents. Before he left this time, he called. "My father got a better job for more money in the Boston area. We'll probably be moving away before the July Fourth weekend." I couldn't believe it. Life without Caleb. His goofy smile with his large white teeth beaming in my face. I could spot his freckles a mile away. His ecstatic races after toads and digs for worms in the woods close to his house. Our sleigh rides down the vacant golf course in the winter. Baking chocolate-chip cookies together and having flour fights. Who would I build a blanket tent with, or read next to without ever having to say a word? Or mold a fort out of snow with? When I was four, my mother had called it "parallel play." Caleb and I had perfect parallel play. Except when he got a little bossy. And I got a little stubborn. So we were equal partners.

"You can't move." I stopped suddenly short of more words.

"I am," he said sadly.

His voice sounded so final, there was nothing more to say. Inside, I felt so alone.

The Easter Sunday that Caleb was in Wellesley, we went to Grandma Fanny's for a Passover Seder. David fell asleep halfway through the Haggadah reading, but at least he got a chance, since he was the youngest, to ask The Four Questions. After the meal, which seemed endless, we helped my grandmother clear away the table, fill the teapot with water, and wait for the coffee to brew. Grandma threw her apron off, wiped her hands on the dishtowel, and turned to me. "Darling, how would you like to take a walk? Just the two of us."

I felt surprised because that was something I had done only with Grandpa. "Sure," I said, grabbing my dungaree jacket as I watched Grandma arrange the mandlebrot and sponge cake on the dessert plate.

"We'll be back soon," she yelled into the small dining area. "I need some fresh air. Watch the coffee pot near the stove." Grandma winked at me as I followed her out the screen door down the front stoop toward the street. "So, how's life treating you?" she asked.

"I guess Mom told you what happened in school with my violin."

"Such a _shande_."

I looked up at Grandma. The light made her hair look silver.

"A shame, darling. A real shame."

124

"I got another violin. A rented one. It's not good. There's a small selection toward the end of the year. Even at the beginning of the school year, there aren't many that sound too great."

"I wish I had a ton of money to buy you a wonderful one!" She touched the side of my cheek. Her finger followed the line of my jaw.

"A Guarneri del Gesù?" I looked into her hazel-colored eyes.

"Or a Stradivarius," she teased back. "The next time I have an extra million dollars lying around, I'll think of you, darling."

"Thanks, Gram."

"Anytime." She squeezed my shoulder. "Zip up. It's breezy."

I tugged at my zipper. "It's stuck. I'm warm enough."

"Come on, I'm not returning damaged goods," she insisted.

Grandma sighed as we looked up at the stars and the moonlight that melted into the sea behind the dunes. "Grandpa and I loved to take walks after dinner."

"I miss him." I jammed my knuckles into my jacket pockets.

"I miss him, too," she said. "I have you. You're a part of him. So are your father and David. You're all little versions of him. Your dad has his blue eyes, David has his smile, and you have his patience."

"What else?"

"Grandpa's gift for music, in a way. He never took a lesson, but he could play Beethoven's Moonlight Sonata by ear."

"He played that without being able to read music?"

"His sisters got the lessons. He only did it by ear. I never heard them play a note. Grandpa used to come home from work and would play after dinner for quite a while sometimes to relax."

"Wow," I said, thinking of the piano in the corner of Grandma's living room covered with a lace tablecloth, candlesticks, and a glass candy dish that was always filled with chocolate Kisses.

"Maybe talent skips a generation and you got your gift from Grandpa?"

My whole inside felt warm at the thought that Grandpa remained. A lot more of him than his pressed white handkerchiefs.

As we continued to walk, the sky turned to a bright orange.

"Grandma, did Mom or Dad ever tell you about my principal?"

"What about him?" She shivered and placed her hands across her stomach under the bulky sweater she was wearing.

"Well," I paused, wondering if I should tell her. Would she understand? "He's dying of AIDS."

Grandma looked at me. "You mean he's *living* with AIDS."

I stared at her, surprised.

"When Grandpa got cancer, everyone fell apart, including me. Every day I tried to block out of my mind the fact that he was going to die. I had to hold on to what I had left of him, and that was life. He was alive for however long he was going to be with me. I could talk to him, watch a Marx Brothers movie with him, laugh, eat a meal with him when he could eat, and lie down next to him and hold on. Hold on to life, Jason. I loved Grandpa more than anything in the world. In a very different way than I love all you kids. Grandpa and I shared a lot. He really valued a good joke. And music. And my cooking. I guess me, in general. I'll never feel the same way in the world without him."

"Mom would say you're not a feminist," I teased.

"I was a woman deeply in love. Period."

"Some of the kids at school are so mean about Mr. Carr."

"People aren't always very sensitive to each other. Let me tell you about my cousin Benny. Fifty years ago, talk had it in the family that Benny was a little," she hesitated, "different."

"Different?" I asked. "How?"

"Some relatives would whisper to one another that he was a *fagelah*. Not a nice term for a homosexual." She lowered her voice. "To me, Benny was Benny. He was my cousin and I loved him. Inside and out. When Benny and I were old enough to go out alone, sometimes he'd bring a friend along, and the three of us would go to a Sunday matinee at the movies and to Chinatown afterward and share a huge dinner. And when you were born, he didn't have a lot of money, but he sent a small check and planted a tree in Israel in your name as a baby gift. Somewhere in Jerusalem, you could be fruitful in olives or dates. Did we hear from any of the other cousins? Not on your life. So don't talk to me about people. Be nice to him, your principal."

"I am," I said.

"Good boy," she said as we made a full circle back to her house.

May

After the vacation Caleb and I didn't see as much of each other as we used to. I was busy with the end of Hebrew school, preparing for the last year before my Bar Mitzvah, and Caleb spent weekends with his parents looking for new places to live near Boston, packing, or getting rid of stuff he no longer needed. One night he asked over the telephone, "Want my old fish tank with the two big fish, and a breeder in the corner filled with tadpoles? My mother said, 'I'm not driving up the New England Thruway with two dogs, a cat, three kids, and ten gallons of water.'"

"I'll ask my parents," I said, hoping they'd say yes.

One night my mother glanced up from the middle of making artichoke hearts with roasted shitake mushrooms and Tuscan peppers while I was in the foyer warming up my fingers with my three octave scales.

"How's Caleb?" she asked innocently.

"How should I know? What am I, his mother?"

My mother paused, seeding a pepper. "Just asking. I hope you two didn't have a fight. You should treasure these last few weeks."

I didn't want to admit that I was angry with him for leaving. I knew I was being stupid. But I wasn't the only one. Lately, Caleb hardly ever called anymore. Was he pulling back, slowly leaving town, afraid to say good-bye? I knew I'd miss him. I had known him since nursery school. I'd never had another friendship like I had with him. It seemed as though I was saying good-bye to Grandpa, to Sniffles, to Mr. Carr, and now to Caleb. Mom and Dad told me eventually I'd be stronger if I "weathered the emotions." I felt weaker from the losses.

As I watched my mother remove the pepper seeds, I thought of the day Caleb and I had gotten an A on our science project. "Can I have the seeds? Maybe Caleb and I could plant them."

With a smile, Mom shoved them off the cutting board and into a plastic bag for me.

At the first chamber music practice after the spring break, Mr. Andrews announced, "Alexandra Wheaten will be our soloist. Everyone in this room is a good musician, and tried, that's what counts."

"Not really," I heard someone behind me whisper.

"I expected it," Shihung said. "Didn't you?" he asked me. I nodded. "So neither of us will be in the limelight," he added.

"Alexandra is very talented," I said.

"There will always be someone better," he said, "but one day each of us will be in a situation where we are the better one, right?"

"Right," I answered him with the same optimism he showed, though a part of me had hoped a miracle could have happened and I could have gotten the solo. Inside, I was very disappointed after the months of anticipation. All that work, and for what? Maybe I should give it all up? Maybe I didn't belong in the recital? Maybe someone was trying to tell me something when my violin got smashed: that in the end this all wasn't meant to be. Who was I kidding? There was no way I even had a chance after my violin was smashed. Was it the violin, or was it me? Mr. Carr would have had an answer. I wished I did.

The night of the Chamber Music Recital, Caleb called. "Break a leg," he said into the receiver. "Not a string!"

It was good hearing his voice again. "Thanks," I said, feeling like old times.

"I'll be out there in the dark, listening."

In that indistinct ocean of darkness, the audience is a blur. I'd close my eyes, forget them, and play. But could I?

My parents dropped me off at the side door of the auditorium. My father was holding the tripod and video camera he had bought when I was born. David was carrying the extension cord. They rarely take videos, except when I play, at birthday parties, or if David does something cute in the bathtub that is usually pretty dumb.

"Good luck!" Dad beamed.

"I love you," my mother whispered.

"I'll clap," David added. "Loud."

I couldn't smile, because I was nervous. I walked in the direction of several groups waiting in the wings offstage. Before a performance I need to be alone, inside my own head, away from my family. Quiet. Calm. Because I'm not. Reiko grinned and handed me a program as I joined the others. Our place was third. That wasn't bad. I hated going on first. By the end, the audience has forgotten you. Last, I would have to wait through all the other pieces as I listened to others make mistakes or sound wonderful. Out of seven groups, plus the solo, third was a good position.

My hands began to perspire as I heard Mr. Andrews introduce the Chamber Music Recital. "I want to thank everyone for coming tonight. My parents schlepped me for bassoon lessons. My grandparents did the same for my parents. I know you do the same." The audience laughed and I wondered if Reiko, Minsoo, and Shihung understood, because they laughed as well. Then Mr.

Andrews leaned into the microphone, which made a piercing screech, and everyone held their ears. "Hope that didn't harm anyone's hearing. We have a great program tonight." He apologized, rested his arms on the podium, and cleared his throat. "The school system offers an instrument to every child in third grade. We are fortunate to have an administration that supports music, and a community who pays the taxes enabling this program to exist. We are also lucky to have a dedicated educator like Mr. Carr, who can't be here tonight but will be with us in spirit." I agreed as I stood safely behind the curtain, listening. Otherwise, I wouldn't be standing here tonight with a violin at my side. I decided to play my heart out for him.

My chest throbbed as the first ensemble went on. They were nine seventh-graders in a combination of wind and string instruments. I barely heard the second group. When it was our turn to go on, I followed the pink satin bow in Reiko's hair to the middle of the stage. We sat down and tuned our instruments. The spotlights overhead were hot and made me feel even warmer than I already was. My insides trembled a little as the accompanist played A on the piano. We watched the pianist, nodded gently to each other, and began, together, in sync, like one person. At first my head was swimming, trying to follow. Then the sounds captured me until I became a part of the ebb and flow of the music as we moved to each other's rhythms in a magical dance. Minsoo's long black skirt was draped behind her cello like a hammock, swaying as her body moved. Shihung was right. I love performing. I was startled by the burst of applause after the final note. As fast as it had begun, it was over. The excitement. The heat. The sounds. They were invigorating and tiring at the same time.

"We did good." Shihung put his hand face up. "Slip me five," he said as we walked backstage.

I slid my palm across his. "This was fun."

"Maybe we'll jam together sometime," he teased, putting his viola and bow away into his case.

"I'd like that." As the words came out, I thought, I really would. Then, Alexandria passed by. "You were great," I said.

"Thank you." She smiled modestly, rushing toward her parents.

"It will be your turn, too," Shihung leaned over and whispered in my ear. "Someday, you'll remember that I told you so."

When the concert was finally finished, my parents pushed past other proud parents congratulating each other. David yawned, since it was way past his bedtime. He came alive when I asked, "Could we go to the Scoop Shoppe? Can Caleb come?"

"The car was heading in that direction before you asked," my father said, jingling the car keys.

I ran over to Caleb. "Want to come for some ice cream?"

Caleb's mother smiled and said, "Go. Enjoy yourself."

Concert nights, Henry and everyone else who worked at the ice-cream parlor always seemed to wonder why there was a run on hot fudge in the middle of the week. Barney and his mother were already standing at the counter when we got inside and headed toward the back of the line. He turned around and saw Caleb and me. Instinct told me to wave to him as someone I knew, then my brain remembered who it was, so I left my arm dangling, pretending I didn't see him. Mrs. Rosenthal weaved her way through the crowd toward a round marble table in the corner as she balanced her banana split. She paused when she noticed my mother. "By the way, Evan Carr has been given two years of medical coverage. With the cost of health insurance, that was quite generous."

"What if he needs more than two years? Is there a time clock on life?" My mother moved with the line as it edged closer to the cash register.

"Let's be realistic, Lauren."

"Yes, let's be. The man is gravely ill."

"Exactly. He'll be lucky if he's even around a year."

My mother bit her bottom lip, turned away from Mrs. Rosenthal, and looked at the high school girl scooping cones. "May I have a mocha chip ice-cream soda with coffee syrup, please?" She said it sweetly, but I could tell Mom was fuming inside as her head drooped down and my father grabbed her hand, tightly, stroking her fingers with his.

When my family finally found an empty booth and sat down, Caleb took a small package from the pocket of his flannel shirt and handed it to me. "I thought you would like these for your bedroom ceiling."

I peeked inside and found some tiny white stars that had a pale green glow. "Save them for your new room," I said, handing them back. "I have plenty of constellations mapped out. Any more, the glow will keep me awake at night."

"But you were missing Orion's Belt," he said. "Keep them."

I looked up and knew then and there that no matter what, even if we didn't see each other for years, Caleb and I would always be friends.

Mrs. Jackson held a piece of thick stationery as we filed into the classroom. When we were seated, she said, "I've received a letter from Mr. Carr." There was a sudden hush. "I'd like to share it with you."

> *Dear Mrs. Jackson,*
> *I was extremely impressed by the quality of writing in the beautifully bound book I received recently. The poetry and the accompanying artwork came together to create a*

successful total effect. I appreciate that the children thought of me. I will always value this project. Tell them it will take an important place in my library. Right now, it is at my bedside, and I enjoy picking it up and glancing through the pages. Knowing my students remain nearby is comforting.

Your principal,

Evan Carr

Nobody said a word. Mrs. Jackson tucked the letter inside the envelope. "I'm going to save this note from Mr. Carr for any of you who would like to see it. I'm putting it next to your reports." I was a little disappointed that Mr. Carr had written to the class and not to me, but it was better than nothing.

Wendy dabbed her eyes under her glasses with a tissue. The rest of the day, the mood in the classroom was quiet until Barney accidentally spilled some liquid plant fertilizer next to Mrs. Jackson's African violet onto the letter from Mr. Carr. "Sorry," he shouted, "I needed a pencil. I didn't mean to, honest. Sorry," he repeated.

Caleb and I looked at each other and just shook our heads.

"I'll leave it in the afternoon sun. Please, everyone, be careful." She placed the leaf of paper on a clear spot on the windowsill, under one of the rocks that Caleb had brought in during the year. The slight breeze and the sun's warmth dried it near the half-open window.

Later that afternoon, before dinner, Caleb showed up with a huge bag of shards of colored glass pebbles. "They look like emeralds." I said, examining them.

"These are for you," he said, "when you set up the fish tank and put my fish in. We found a new house, and my parents are making the move official over Memorial Day weekend. They're signing some papers."

I swallowed the lump in my throat. "I don't remember the names of your fish." I poked at the pebbles as they cascaded over my fingers.

"I never named them. They don't come when you call, Jason."

"Still," I said, "everyone should have a name."

"When you lift the lid of the tank, they swim together to the top, waiting to be fed. They like the purple fluorescent light at night."

"I'm going to name them Goldie and Lox."

"Goldilocks? For two fish?" he said, sounding surprised.

"Goldie and *Lox*," I said definitively.

"Oh," Caleb moaned. "Don't eat them."

"Only with bagels and cream cheese on Sunday morning. Just kidding. They're safe!" I stared at the green pebbles. "Well," I said, "thanks again, Caleb. I'll take good care of your fish. I promise.

And of course you have visiting privileges any time."

He lingered a moment, staring at the glistening pebbles, too.

After Caleb left, I felt lonely. Knowing his fish would be here in about a month or so made the move seem real. I carried the bag into my room and wrote a letter to Mr. Carr, something I hadn't done in a while. Now that he'd written to the class, maybe he'd finally write to me?

> *Dear Mr. Carr,*
>
> *I wanted to tell you how the Chamber Music Recital went, but then I decided I don't have to. Instead, my father made an extra copy of the tape he made the night of the concert, so you can judge for yourself. I hope you enjoy seeing everyone. Or should I say, hearing us. I am sorry that you couldn't be there in person. As you can see, I didn't get the solo, but I'll try next year, and keep trying until maybe I get it!*
>
> *On to other news. Before Memorial Day weekend this year, we are going to have "Specials Week." I know you liked to do it in March, but time slipped away, and without you, somehow the week didn't get organized. This year, everyone voted to do activities for one whole week relating to the environment. Ms. Mosely wants everyone to do projects on "How to Save the Planet." She announced*

*over the PA, "Use the three R's: Reduce.
Reuse. Recycle."*

*We've hoarded candy wrappers, freezer
foil from hamburgers (say that five times
fast), roasting pans (hold the grease, yuck!),
leftover bulletin board decorations, pie
plates, you name it! We searched through our
lunch bags, mining through juice boxes and
used pudding cups to find anything remotely
silver and shiny. Barney Rosenthal nearly
grabbed Wendy Weins's saliva-slicked
retainer by mistake, which was resting on a
soggy napkin while she munched carrot
sticks at lunch. I guess he was desperate.*

*The fifth grade is using recycled foil
products to construct a Knight in Shining
Armor for their upcoming Medieval Festival
and Renaissance Fair. The last day in the
cafeteria, the plan is to roll out the largest
ball of aluminum foil anyone has ever seen
for the Reynolds Aluminum Company's contest called "Great Balls of Foil." (Instead of
the song "Great Balls of Fire." Get it? Ha.
Ha.). I'll keep you posted on the event. Too
bad you're missing this, too. I know you
would have contributed something wild and
crazy to this week.*

Best wishes,

Jason Glass

P.S. The letter got tucked under my math textbook while I was doing my homework, so I forgot to mail it right away. This gives me a chance to fill you in on the outcome of the week's events.

Tommy Wachowski's father backed his van to the rear doors of the caf and brought the aluminum ball to the recycling plant at the town dump. It's weight almost equaled a newborn elephant. We thought it would be eligible for a $100 cash prize for our school for the largest ball, until we lost to a middle school on the South Shore of Long Island. Word on the street is that some Styrofoam found its way into their ball, but who knows for sure? No one's going to challenge them and sift through garbage.

Tommy's dad said that there was so much metal, he was considering using it in his plumbing business, but I doubt a pie plate pipe would hold up in a bathroom or a kitchen.

Have a good Memorial Day weekend!

June

❦

When we returned after the four-day weekend, Mrs. Jackson looked strange. She always stands near the doorway of the classroom to welcome us each morning. Today she was seated at her desk, holding the stained letter from Mr. Carr that had dried off wrinkled. "Sit down, everyone," she said before Ms. Mosely came on the PA system to say the pledge. "I have"—her voice weakened—"I have something disturbing to say. Mr. Carr died suddenly last evening of complications from his illness. I heard about it this morning when I came into school." Wendy started to cry. Mrs. Jackson went to Wendy's side and put her arm around her shoulders, which moved up and down as she sobbed. "I imagine many of you feel as shocked as I was to hear this, but we'll go through this together. I'm here for all of you." When I glanced across the table from my desk, I saw Tommy's eyes red and swollen. This surprised me more than anything. Maybe even more than Mr. Carr dying. Did this remind him of his mother's death? I guess you never know about people.

Mrs. Jackson said, "I don't feel like doing work today. I imagine none of you do, either. Maybe we should do something that would have made Mr. Carr happy? And that makes everyone in this room happy inside. Let's give ourselves some joy today. I think that's how we'll remember him best." That's when we came up with the idea for a time capsule. She put on some classical music in the background, and this is how I began.

> *Dear Mr. Carr,*
>
> *Mrs. Jackson gave us an assignment. She said, "Since you're the graduating class of Sherman Elementary School, I want you to think of how you would all like to be remembered one hundred years from now. Close your eyes. Pretend your great-grandchildren attend this school. They are going to open a time capsule that they will dig up in the school yard. Inside they will find what you felt about our school, a teacher, or an event that happened here. You can express yourself any way that you wish."*
>
> *Tommy Wachowski joked, "I'm leaving Thursday's pizza. Or maybe Friday's lentil soup, which smells like the bottom of my sneakers after gym. The landfill in the sandpits will smell like candy compared to the brew in that*

capsule. Bless my olfactory nerves!" (We're studying sense of smell in our science unit.)

Wendy Weins, who is always so-o serious, announced, "I'm donating a copy of Romeo and Juliet." (She read that for our Super Bowl Reading Club and got over twenty footballs for reading an extra thirty minutes every night.) Barney Rosenthal is donating his mother's PTA speeches, which everyone is tickled pink about. My best friend, Caleb, is encasing a section of his butterfly and bug collection that he has had pinned to a corkboard over the slop sink in the back of the classroom. He's considering the addition of a few of his favorite rocks, which he found on a trip to the Delaware River Water Gap. I think the rocks will make it too heavy.

I've decided to write about you for the time capsule. I think (and hope) you wouldn't have minded. The worst part is that I'm writing you a letter too late, and that you won't be at the ceremony when we put everyone's stuff inside the capsule. It just won't be the same without you. What I want to say is how sorry I am you died of a terrible disease, and by the time the capsule is opened, I wish that there will be a cure for AIDS. I hope one hundred years from now no one will even know what I am talking about. We are making a wish list in class. I already have thirteen. My fourteenth wish would be this, and it would be a lucky number! When I was little, I had made a "Claw Counter-Potion Formula 70" to cure you of the condi-

144

tion you said you got during a full moon when your toenails became claws. I wish my belief in potions could be as simple now as it had been in second grade.

I remember when the letter was first sent home—that you weren't coming back after the winter recess, and how awful I felt. I kept staring at it next to my milk and cookies. Eventually, we were told that you had a long illness and due to health reasons you thought it best to resign. Cold and flat. Nothing else. Some parents at PTA meetings whispered or made a fuss, but no one who really knew you listened. I still think they should have told us the real truth. So here goes:

This is the truth about my principal, Mr. Carr. He realized that someday I wanted to be a violinist and encouraged me to audition for the school system's Chamber Music Recital. All the parents were there the night I played. My knees were shaking so much, I nearly fell off the stage. I'll never forget that.

Instead of dull assemblies, he once had a mime come to the school. As Mr. Carr made a speech over the microphone introducing the act, the mime mimicked him behind his back while the entire student body laughed. And Mr. Carr knew. He deliberately continued, so the laughter escalated to a roaring thunder. We wore black and painted our faces white. The gym was a mob scene. Everyone spent a few days pretending to pour glasses of water in midair, climbing up staircases that weren't there, or opening and walking through imaginary doors.

One rainy day during lunch, Mr. Carr showed old black-and-white movies of Laurel and Hardy. I laughed so hard, the milk I was drinking shot out of my nose onto my best friend, Caleb's, sandwich. Another time, Mr. Carr recited nonsense poetry by Lewis Carroll over the loudspeaker. Also on the PA system, he played the radio recording of H. G. Wells's War of the Worlds. *I was scared, but I went home and read the book. After I was done, I did a diorama of green clay monsters (my brother, David, rolled the fangs) and I spray-painted the background fluorescent-pink. When Mr. Carr saw it hanging in the hall, he said that I was inspired!*

Mr. Carr had a guinea pig, named Mr. Hobbs, that lived in his office. In the corner of the hutch on top of the wood chips was a little mat that he stretched out on. Everyone took turns taking him home. I won a turn during a winter vacation. Mr. Carr called from Puerto Rico, where he was visiting a college roommate, to find out how he was doing. I said, "My father's bringing home leftovers from the restaurant for him: endive, watercress, pineapple slices." Mr. Carr said, "He'll never want to leave!" But I knew Mr. Hobbs missed Mr. Carr's pats and scratches behind his ears. Mr. Hobbs eventually had a family. Mr. Carr would have liked seeing all the little baby guinea pigs.

Mr. Carr was a special principal and person because he cared about the children more than sucking up to the parents or pleasing the administration. If a student was sick and their parents worked and no one could pick them up, he would run to the deli across the street from the playground and buy chicken soup. I once had to go to the office with a message and saw him reading a picture book to a kindergartner in the nurse's cubicle as the girl sipped a cup of steaming soup. It fogged up her eyeglasses so much, he spoonfed her the noodles. As my mother once said to me, "The small acts in life are what count. Not the big splashy ones." I'm going to plant an extra tulip for Mr. Carr in the garden he planted for Patrick Shutler after he had died. A red one that stands out in the middle of the sea of white ones. I doubt they'll be growing by the time the capsule is opened, but who knows? My mother says, "Miracles can happen."

I guess what I really need to say is: Mr. Carr, if you could have put something in the capsule, what would it have been? A vaccine? A cure? If there was one. Knowing you, it probably would have been something showing all of us about you, like the yearbook picture we took at the beginning of September under the flagpole. You sent in your baby photo! The whole graduating class decided we're going to do the same. I have one of me wearing a bib that says GUCCI GOO *on it. I'm sitting in an antique high*

chair and I have creamed spinach all over my
chubby cheeks. I hope someday that my children
are lucky enough to have a teacher or principal
in their life like you. So in a way, you are not
entirely gone. You'll always be a part of me and
live on like a time capsule, maybe with no end.

Your student and friend,

Jason Glass

The following day, I returned Tommy's baseball mitt to him.

"I found it," I said to him when we were the
last two left in the school yard.

He stared at the mitt for a while, rubbing his
thumb over the dried leather. "Where?"

"Around," I answered. "Is it important
where?"

Tommy shrugged. "Maybe. Maybe not."

"As long as you've got it, right?"

"Yeah, I guess so. But, Glass, why did you
return it? You think I ruined your violin. I'm not
stupid."

"I think you put Barney up to it. He had the
opportunity. He has a reason to be in the orchestra
room where the violins are stored during the day;
you don't. And Barney is weak. You know what I've
learned? I'm strong. Maybe you can destroy my
instrument, but if I give in to hate, then it will
destroy me. And what kind of player will I become?

If I've learned anything from Mr. Carr dying, it's that he died without anger. He died with courage. My violin can be scarred. I can't."

Tommy looked at me. He didn't move. He said nothing.

"People don't always get what they want. I didn't get the solo. For a while I blamed you and Barney. Now I have hope for other solos, other years. Hope will keep me trying. Without it, there's nothing. And Mr. Carr kept going without hope."

"Hope? My mother died without any." Tommy sounded numb.

I put my arm on his shoulder. He kicked a rock across the dirt. I realized I'd never get the truth about my violin. It was no longer important.

The day of graduation, Caleb walked next to me as we filed down the center aisle two by two to receive our diplomas from Ms. Mosely. "It's weird not having Mr. Carr hand us the certificate after all these years," I whispered to Caleb before it was our turn. I looked out on the mass of faces and picked out my parents, my brother, my grandmother, then Mrs. Jackson and Miss Ryan. Ms. Mosely gave me a special music certificate. Mr. Carr's printed signature remained at the bottom, and seeing it there made me smile. I thought about the wishes on my list, and how one of my first ones was *Come back, Mr. Carr. Please.* Maybe he was watching us now?

"I'm going to miss this joint," Tommy mumbled as we stood on the platform, waiting for the last names.

"Me, too," Caleb said, nudging me in the side.

When Ms. Mosely came to Zachary Ziefloffer, there were whistles and applause and shouts. Finally we had gotten to the end, to reach a new beginning. Grandma gave me a great big hug that nearly squashed me to death. "I wouldn't have missed this for the world. I'm all *fahklempte.*"

"Choked up inside with emotion," Mom said, beaming.

"I'm feeling *fahklempte,* too," Dad added, hugging me and Grandma.

"So am I." David looked up at me.

As we all hugged and kissed, me a little less in public, I noticed Barney and his mother. His father hadn't shown up, and for the first time, I felt bad for him.

When Caleb's family moved, I couldn't watch the vans take his furniture away. We had pizza the night before, amid the packed cartons of books and dishes. My parents promised me that we'd drive up to Boston on Labor Day weekend. Caleb and I wanted to see the Aquarium with its tanks of coral reefs, tropical saltwater fish, and penguins.

I wrote a song for Caleb to the tune of "Jingle Bells."

> *Splashing to and fro*
> *Amoebas like to play*
> *In a plastic petri dish*
> *Dividing all the day.*
>
> *I thought there were two,*
> *When I first explored,*
> *But looked through a microscope*
> *And counted up to four.*
>
> *Chorus*
> *Single cells, single cells,*
> *See how they divide,*
> *There was one on Labor Day*
> *And now it multiplied.*

Several days later after Caleb was gone and I was waiting to leave for music camp, I received a letter from Mr. Carr. For a few minutes I just held the envelope in my hands. I had been waiting so long, and now I was almost afraid to open it. When I did, I noticed it had been written a few days before he died. It had gotten lost in the mail. Tears dripped onto the blue stationery and I wiped them off with the bottom of my T-shirt before the ink got smudged. I could have written him back before he died and sent him the letter in the time capsule instead of the one I wrote about dumb recycling. I felt awful. Again, I thought about how strange it was not seeing him at graduation. I felt honored that he had thought of me and taken the time to write. Mr. Carr had signed it at the bottom. His

151

handwriting was kind of wobbly, sort of like David's.

> *Dear Jason,*
>
> *You have been a very good friend to me these last several months. I have truly looked forward to receiving your letters as you kept me tuned in to all the goings-on about our school. You children were such an important part of my life. At times, I missed that so. Even the smell of the lentil soup on Fridays! I am especially sorry that I missed your May debut at the celebrated Chamber Music Recital. I heard you did very well before you sent the tape, which pleased me greatly. Thank you for the recording of Vivaldi's* **Four Seasons.** *So you played "Spring." How very fitting for the concert. The music's on in the background as this is being written. I find it very comforting. Though sometimes, Jason, I need some Billie Holiday and New Orleans jazz. My Cajun friend has influenced and spoiled me.*
>
> *I know Mrs. Jackson has been having the class make a list of things you may want or need in life. I haven't lived long enough, but I've seen a lot and come up with a few to pass on so that maybe yours will be a full life. I think you've started already. Okay, here goes:*
>
> 1) *We all need a muse: a spirit, an inspiration to bring out the poetry, the art, the music. You've found yours in the violin at*

such a young age. I'm glad the school was here to help you discover it—to offer you an instrument. I feel in some small way, I was a part of your muse. Thank you.

2) Enjoy the people you love and care about (and pets too!). Hug them and kiss them and tell them how you feel. Take the time. Time goes by quickly. Grab life. Take it under your wings. And soar.

3) Tell a lot of jokes every day. Especially at dinnertime. It's fun to laugh and eat. Don't choke, though. Laughter will help you live a better life. Certainly it will help you get through hard times, which no one is spared. Here's a joke about living a long time:

An old man goes to get an insurance policy.

The agent asks, "How old are you?"

"Seventy-nine," the man answers.

The broker says, "I'm sorry, but you're too old."

The man says, "You gave my father one just last week."

"Your father? How old's your father?"

"A hundred and five."

"A hundred and five!"

The agent looks up the father's name. Sure enough, a policy was issued and his father was in perfect health. The agent comes back and says, "I apologize. You're right. Come in next Monday for a medical exam, and we'll give you insurance."

"I can't."

"Why not?"

"My grandfather's getting married."

"Your grandfather?" The agent is shocked.

"What can I say, his parents keep pestering him."

4) Eat healthy foods. If you must cheat, these are my favorites: fried chicken and whipped potatoes with thick, warm gravy; spicy dumplings and spare ribs; cheese enchiladas and chimichangas in green sauce with sour cream; teriyaki; udon noodles with shrimp tempura; pakoras; gyros; and lasagna. These are a few just to begin with. I'm sure since your parents own a restaurant, you could educate me on a few dishes.

5) Get a good night's sleep. I never realized how important that is until I couldn't get one. You'll be more cheerful to face the day. Trust me on this one. I'm not trying to be a grown-up. Don't feel funny about taking your own pillow with you when you travel or sleep at a friend's. Who cares? As long as you're happy.

6) Be connected with the earth. Now I know this sounds "in" and popular, but since I was a small boy, my father bought me seeds and let me plant them in my own

space in the garden each spring. We'd get a bale of peat moss and really do a number on the vegetable plot. I always loved getting my bare feet on the freshly cut grass (even though I was allergic!) and my toes in the soil, and rolling down the hill of our front lawn. Also, if you can, live close to the water. It's soothing. That's why I loved being a principal in our town. Every day when I went to work, I passed by the bay and the duck pond, and felt happy to be alive. Sounds corny, but true.

7) *Since you told me that seven is your lucky number, I'll end here. Because someone once said to me that life is like a throw of the die. And you know what? A lot of it is just plain luck. That doesn't mean I don't want you to try and work hard, but have faith in fate, luck, whatever you want to call it. I can even still say that now. Because if we don't believe in something—some hope, some dream— what else is there? That's what I'd wish for you, Jason, if you were my own child—an endless pocketful of luck and skill so that you fulfill your dreams, and that they're not unfinished dreams, so life on earth becomes heaven.*

Your friend, always,

Evan Carr

I stared at the letter for several minutes and reread it once again. Then I took out my wish list from the beginning of the year to see if Mrs. Jackson was right about how the things you want in life can change. I finally realized nothing and no one can live forever, no matter how much I prayed they would. Not Grandpa. Or Sniffles. Or Mr. Carr. Mr. Carr's life wasn't a tragedy, because he did live long enough to pass joy on to other people, to me. Patrick Shutler's death was a tragedy. "It was a life not fully realized, before dreams could become fulfilled," Mr. Carr had said at the memorial assembly. Mr. Carr inspired me to realize mine, through music.

I erased the wish about Mr. Carr coming back. That would never be. As I headed for another summer, wishing summer had lasted longer a year ago, I realized I'd never again do laps in the town pool next to Mr. Carr. I smiled, remembering the ducks on his bathing suit. I couldn't bring anything back. Sometimes I'd get all choked up thinking of Sniffles. I guess I'd have to take life day by day.

As far as Tommy being in my class, he hurts himself more than anyone. Even if he and Barney are in some of my classes in junior high, I won't care. They have to live with what they did. I know they did it.

I'd add to the list that I wish Caleb hadn't moved. School won't be the same without him. If I've learned anything, it's to go on, but the "on" is in a different way, and sometimes that's painful.

The wish about David disappearing I already took out. I imagine there will be many times when I will want to put it back in, when he makes me real angry. But he's my brother, and I love him.

The wish about Juilliard. That wish would remain.

It was the time of day when the sun is beginning to set and the sky has streaks of pink and orange. Sometimes lavender. Tonight, a blood-red. The doorbell rang. I thought, had Dad forgotten his key again? Then I wondered, why would he be home now? Well, since I was leaving the next morning for six weeks of music camp in Vermont, maybe Dad wanted to be home early and be with me? I peeked through the window curtains billowing in the breeze. A man was standing on the front steps, holding a violin case. Strange, I thought. Mom said, "Never open the door to strangers." I paused, feeling safe with her in the backyard weeding the herb garden and picking tarragon for dinner tonight. Was this person a friend of Mrs. Lee, my violin teacher? Luckily, Mom came to the side near the driveway, squinting in the sunlight. She shielded her eyes with her hand as he introduced himself. I heard their muffled voices through the screen door.

"Jason," my mother said, "this is Mr. Carr's friend. I'll let him tell you why he's here."

I looked at my mother tentatively, wondering what was going on. He looked the same age as Mr. Carr. Over forty, under fifty. I only knew kids' ages perfectly.

"Jason." The man stepped forward and put out his hand to shake mine. "I've been looking forward to meeting you."

"You have?" I said.

He nodded. "Ever since your letters started arriving at Evan's."

"Ah huh," I said, feeling confused. "I thought those letters were between him and me. I never meant for anyone else to read them."

"He was a close friend. He shared them with me. I hope you don't mind."

I wasn't sure whether I did or not. He seemed nice enough, like my father with his blue eyes, and brown hair graying near his temples. He had friendly eyes that twinkled. Eyes that wouldn't hurt anyone.

"Anyway," he continued, "Evan wanted you to have this."

I stepped back, shocked, without extending my arm. "A violin?"

"His violin."

"*His* violin? He played?"

The man smiled as if remembering. "Yes, he played. Played well."

"How well?" I asked, wondering if I were being too forward. But this was the time to ask—I'd never get another chance.

"Well enough to have gone to Juilliard, and visit Russia to sit in on the Tchaikovsky Competition."

"Juilliard's my dream."

He shoved the case toward me. "It's yours."

"I couldn't." I shivered inside.

"He truly wanted you to have it. It's not the best fiddle around, but he said, 'If Jason can get a decent Tchaikovsky someday out of this, he deserves it.'"

My eyes welled up with tears.

"Finish his dreams. Okay?" the man said.

"Okay." I smiled, accepting the violin. "I'll try my best."

I was about to ask him his name and thank him, but he turned very suddenly and quickly walked away. I think he was crying, too.

My mother sat down next to me. I put my head on her shoulder. She squeezed me, sighed, and tapped the beat-up violin case. "Should we hear how it sounds?"

"Why not?" I said, excited, curious.

We went inside. I rested the case on the floor and opened the lid. The inside was a smooth burgundy velvet, and the violin was wrapped in a silk paisley scarf. As I lifted the scarf, the wood smelled of polish and the nylon strings of alcohol. Someone had cleaned it not long ago. Had Mr. Carr played it recently? Before he died? Or had his friend done this for me? I closed my eyes and took a deep breath, opened them, and then gently cradled the instrument toward my chin. My heart raced. I tuned the violin. Then I tucked one of Grandpa's white handkerchiefs under my chin, adjusting myself to the chin rest, ready to begin. For you, Mr. Carr, I thought. I got a chill as I began, knowing he had once played this very violin inside a practice room at Juilliard. Under the roof of Lincoln Center. Maybe in a master class of some famous violinist? Now he wanted it all for me. For my fingers to play vibrato and touch where his had once been. Soar, I thought, as the first notes sounded. Soar.

From the Memorial Service during Yom Kippur
in the Maḥzor, a special prayerbook.

There is a time for all things under the sun:
A time to be born and a time to die
A time to laugh and a time to cry
A time to dance and a time to mourn
A time to seek and a time to lose
A time to forget and a time to remember.
Ecclesiastes III

This day we remember those who enriched our life
with love and with beauty, with kindness and compassion,
with thoughtfulness and understanding.